THE WIZARD'S BAKERY

Gu Byeong-mo was born in 1976 in Seoul. She studied Korean language and literature at Kyung-Hee University. She made her literary debut with the novel *The Wizard's Bakery* (2009). It became a bestseller in Korea and was translated into numerous languages. She has published more than twenty works of fiction and won notable literary prizes.

Jamie Chang is a literary translator. She has translated *Concerning My Daughter* by Kim Hye-jin and *Kim Ji-young, Born 1982* by Cho Nam-joo, among others. She teaches at the Translation Academy at the Literature Translation Institute of Korea.

THE WIZARD'S BAKERY

Gu Byeong-mo

Translated from the Korean
by Jamie Chang

WILDFIRE

위저드 베이커리 by 구병모
Copyright © Gu Byeong-mo 2009
English translation © Jamie Chang 2025

The right of Gu Byeong-mo to be identified as the Author of the
Work has been asserted by her in accordance with the Copyright,
Designs and Patents Act 1988.

First published in the English language in Paperback in 2025 by WILDFIRE,
An Imprint of Headline Publishing Group Limited,
in arrangement with Changbi Publishers, Inc. and Chiara Tognetti Rights
Agency and Korea Copyright Center.

This book is published with the support of the Literature
Translation Institute of Korea (LTI Korea).

1

Cataloguing in Publication Data is available from the British Library

Paperback ISBN 978 1 0354 2804 5

Typeset in 12/15.5pt Bembo MT Pro by Jouve (UK), Milton Keynes

Printed and bound in Great Britain by Clays Ltd, Elcograf S.p.A.

Headline's policy is to use papers that are natural, renewable and recyclable
products and made from wood grown in well-managed forests and other
controlled sources. The logging and manufacturing processes are expected
to conform to the environmental regulations of the country of origin.

Headline Publishing Group Limited
An Hachette UK Company
Carmelite House
50 Victoria Embankment
London EC4Y 0DZ

The authorised representative in the EEA is Hachette Ireland, 8 Castlecourt
Centre, Dublin 15, D15 XTP3, Ireland (email: info@hbgi.ie)

www.headline.co.uk
www.hachette.co.uk

Table of Contents

IMPORTANT NOTE

Please read with care. This book touches on dark topics and sensitive subject matter as follows: domestic violence, grief and loss, sexual assault, physical abuse, rape, suicide/attempted suicide, death of a parent, paedophilia, emotional manipulation, self-harm.

This is a work of magical realism depicting the harsh reality of the society we unfortunately live in, and the consequences of using magic to avoid taking responsibility for one's actions.

Prologue

I smell sugar caramelising over medium heat.

And with that, my senses turn keen: I feel the elasticity of dough freshly kneaded from high-gluten bread flour, hear a pat of yellow butter bubbling into a circle on a frying pan, see the ripples created by a dollop of whipped cream garnishing a cup of coffee. Whenever I stand in front of the bakery, I can feel the yeast at work in the resting dough and make out whether the subtle scent of the tart of the day was fig or apricot.

I am sick of bread.

The 24-hour bakery sat about a hundred yards away from my apartment complex, near the bus stop. I wondered if anyone actually craved a ham croissant or a bland-as-cardboard rosemary bagel at one in the morning, but the place was lit up twenty-four hours a day, ready for customers.

Through the window, I could see a girl around my

age, maybe younger. She worked the register during the day. In the kitchen behind the counter, a man who looked somewhere between late twenties and early thirties baked things that smelled sweet and delicious. At night, the baker shuffled back and forth between the kitchen and the register. As with most small neighbourhood bakeries, the baker appeared to also be the owner.

For a small neighbourhood bakery, they sold an impressive range of baked goods. Each time I passed the place, flour hung in the air and tickled my nose, and I could taste sugar molecules melting on the tip of my tongue. A delivery van pulled up in front of the bakery, loaded a great number of boxes to be shipped out, and drove off.

But the late hours and absurdly large production relative to the size of the establishment were not the only things I found strange about the bakery. The true oddity of the place was the baker. I don't know if that was just my personal opinion or other customers found him strange, too, but I imagine he would have gone out of business much sooner if word had got around the neighbourhood that he was objectively weird.

Provided he kept his mouth shut, the baker looked like any other artisan with a quiet focus on his work: man in a silly-looking paper hat with a ponytail peeking out below, face the colour of finely sifted baking powder. His movements meticulous, graceful and efficient, he looked the part of a skilled pastry chef capable of making a living from word-of-mouth alone, without having to join a franchise. I had always seen him that way as well, until one day when I pointed a pair of tongs at a pastry that sort of resembled a streusel-topped bun but with some questionable modifications, and asked what was in it.

The girl at the register started to say, 'Oats and rye and—'

'Liver. Dried,' a voice interrupted.

I raised my head to see the baker standing in the kitchen doorway, just past the girl's stiffening shoulders.

'Finely ground human infant liver powder. Three parts liver mixed with seven parts flour.'

The tongs slipped out of my hand and hit the floor with a clank. I didn't really believe he had put liver, dried or raw, in the bun. And even if it did contain liver, it would have to be from a pig, and not an infant. (Let's not imagine that unsettling taste.)

But why was he joking about ingredients? It would only be a matter of time before the rumour spread that the neighbourhood baker was a little cuckoo and the Condo Complex Women's Association, concerned about 'harmful establishments' affecting housing prices, would join forces to drive him out.

The girl swatted him on the stomach with the back of her hand and told him to stop joking around.

Of course he was joking. As I sighed and bent down

to pick up the tongs, I spotted wafer cookies on the next shelf. He saw what I was looking at.

'Shit of the titi bird,' he said. 'Spread ever so thinly between two wafers. Glazed with a syrup made from marinated raven eyeballs. They strike a delicate balance between sweet, bitter and sour, rather like Ethiopian coffee . . .'

'Are you trying to drive all of our customers away?' The girl jabbed him in the side.

Was he attempting to make a joke? Why? Just to see how far he would go, I pointed at something that looked like jelly sweets.

'Three-pack of cat tongues. Persian, Siamese, Abyssinian.'

I slammed the tongs on the countertop. The girl took them in the back to wash them, while the baker adjusted his hat and laughed. 'I'm not joking. I was telling you the truth because I thought a child like you would understand.'

Who are you calling a child? Besides, even children these days weren't stupid enough to believe him. Most kids knew that Santa Claus was their parent, their social worker, or some college kid in a santa suit.

I looked around the bakery. The pink-and-yellow chequered wallpaper looked homey. Hanging crookedly on the wall was one of those crudely designed calendars they hand out for free at banks or churches every year. The display case, where the pastry lay in straight rows and columns, was so clean there wasn't a single handprint in sight, and the handle gleamed gold in the light of the overhead lamps. Overall, there was nothing fancy about the place, but it wasn't run-down – no cracks in the walls, and no streams of unidentifiable liquid trickling down the cracks, smelling up the place or giving it a creepy air. It was just your average clean and humble neighbourhood bakery. The baker *looked* normal, too. No matter how hard I searched, nothing about his appearance said he might be a creepy guy despite the things he said.

Stuttering, I asked him if there was anything he could recommend for a normal person to eat, and I grabbed a bag of plain rolls, no sausages or cheese, and set it on the counter. Surely there was nothing in them besides the basic ingredients, like flour, eggs and milk.

But then, as he passed the girl on his way into the kitchen, the baker offered, unsolicited, 'I substituted Rapunzel's dandruff for flour . . .'

I lifted my hand, stopping him before the girl could interject, and put 2,500 won in change on the counter. Assessment complete: the baker is nuts.

I opened the door and stepped outside. Suddenly, I felt as though the dingy neighbourhood bakery was in the middle of a dark forest, the kind that appeared in fairy tales: 'Once upon a time, there was a wizard who lived in a deep, dark forest, and he made different pastries every day. Each time a breeze passed through the forest, the leaves would rustle against each other, passing the scent of those pastries far, far out to the edge of the woods.'

The moment I got home, I would have to tell someone about the place and ask if someone shouldn't do something about the crazy man in the bakery located on the ground floor of the third building from the bus stop . . . but who on earth would I tell?

Returning home and opening the front door, I would confirm that no one was there to listen to me. Wasn't that why I bought the rolls on my way home in the first place? So I could take a bite of bread and a sip of milk, chew on the sentiments of a day that was neither too dry nor too soggy, then store them in an airtight container and pack them away somewhere deep within?

Enough about other people. Who was I to judge whether someone was sane or not? In the eyes of the world, I was probably the loony one, not the man who owns and manages a shop, however small.

My stuttering started four years ago. Reading something out loud, I didn't hesitate or mispronounce words. I could carefully draft my thoughts on paper and read them out loud without any difficulty, but I couldn't produce even a simple yes or no if I didn't have it written in front of me.

Some circuit in my body had to be damaged or infected. Without the medium of written words, my thoughts refused to come out through my mouth. To me, letters were neurotransmitters that stimulated my slow, bumbling synapses. Without putting it down on paper first, my thoughts were not only not my own, but something too trivial even to be called thought, an error message tossed in the recycling bin as soon as it came out of the printer.

If someone were to try to comfort me by saying that everyone finds it hard to think on their feet and string together a coherent sentence, I would agree. But for me, it was more than difficult. It was impossible. No matter how hard I tried, no matter how patiently the other person waited for the words to come, the result was always the same intermittent gasp of repeated consonants and vowels that formed no meaning at all.

The symptoms first appeared at the end of primary school. At first, I couldn't figure out what was going on. Father standing over me and yelling to speak up worsened my fear to the extent that I couldn't take a breath and figure out what was going on in my mouth or in my head. This was a time when people did not understand that stuttering was a mechanical problem that could not be overcome through will-power alone, and they treated stuttering as a symptom of low intelligence.

Not long after I entered middle school, my form

teacher said to me one day, 'Forget it. Just give me a yes or no.'

Despite the very simple options before me, I said yes, then no, then yes, and so on about nine times before he slapped me across the face.

'Yes or no, dammit!'

After a few kicks and a sound whipping, I instinctively curled up into a ball to minimise surface area and potential injury. I was in Teachers' Office 3, a small room occupied by only twelve teachers and no students around to record the brutality with their mobile phone cameras. To this day, I don't recall what the teacher's yes/no question was.

At the end of the year, when I was to be summoned once again by the same form teacher for the annual career counselling, I prepared a piece of paper and a pencil in hope of sparing myself at least one blow. The teacher read my thoughtful, eloquent, logical and, most importantly, scrupulous answer and said he was sorry he had misjudged me before but that I should really see a doctor before I started thinking about my future.

'What's going to happen to you once you go out into the world? You won't even get into university, let alone find a job. No one's going to accept you if you mumble through your interview like the cat's got your tongue. You're all grown up now. You have got to stop dwelling in the past.'

I nodded, while I scoffed to myself, *You think you're so smart, don't you? Putting the pieces together based on what my father told you at parents' evening?* I didn't have to be there to know what he must have said:

'He is my child, but I haven't been a good father to him. Poor thing. His mother abandoned him at Cheongnyangni Station when he was six. We found him a week later! I was so preoccupied with what happened to his mother that I didn't think to look after him, so he had no one . . . I had to enrol him in school early so someone could at least watch him during the day. But now he has a stepmother who provides him with a stable home environment, so if you could just be patient with him . . .'

If the teacher had half a brain, he would have noticed the suspicious time lapse between the abandonment and when my stuttering began, and concluded that the connection between the two was close to nil. (More on this later.)

From then on until I left primary school, none of my teachers ever called on me in class. Even in maths lessons when the answer was just a number, no one, except for a select minority of teachers – some sadistic, others not in the mood to teach – wanted to call on a child who was sure to make the entire class fall behind in the curriculum.

When you have a problem that makes you stick out, you'll be picked on for it. Being of average height with no experience of fighting, I defended myself using a technique I saw once in an illustrated self-defence manual. When someone's beating you, crouch as far down as you can so the attacker's arms are punching vertically. (Be careful not to get too close to the ground, for that's when the kicking starts.) Then grab the attacker's arm and pull straight down, then jump up, shoving their arm up hard. This will dislocate the attacker's shoulder. (Warning: run away as fast as you can while the attacker is screaming in pain, or your joints won't be safe either.)

Father paid for the kid's treatment, and I was suspended for a week. When I returned, the story had snowballed in the absence of the involved parties, and kids started to avoid me. After that, school life was relatively painless. When I got to secondary school, I could publicly announce that I did not speak and not be harassed for it.

The bakery guy and I had something in common – as long as we kept our mouths shut, no one knew that we both had a screw loose somewhere. That was why I was so curious about him and identified with him.

They were coming after me.

The spiral cleats on the bottoms of my sneakers clawed at the ground, rapidly, savagely. The smell of rubber burning from the friction rushed at me. The shrieks, the cries and the fury that clung so tenaciously to my heels, I shook off in the wind.

As I raced down the street, I realised I had nowhere to go. I could spend the night at an internet café or something, but it all happened so quickly that I ran out without grabbing anything. The mobile phone I almost never used (since I don't speak) was still in the bag next to my desk. Not that having the phone on me would have made any difference now. Did I have any 'friends' I could call for help? Would anyone invite me in with open arms and not be frustrated by my stuttering? There was my maternal aunt and grand-mother, but I hadn't heard from them in six years. I didn't know if they were alive or dead, let alone where they lived. How long, and how far could I run like this? I was just about out of ideas when the bakery caught my eye.

I gasped for air. Past the display window dirty with handprints, I could see the baker inside. I had become a regular at the bakery for reasons beyond my control, but if it wasn't for my speech impediment, I would have asked him: *Why is your bakery open twenty-four hours? Does anyone ever come looking for bread this late at night?*

He seemed busy all the time, but even he couldn't be safe from the feelings creeping up in the quiet moments. Wasn't he lonely working there day after day, all by himself? More importantly, when did he sleep?

But thanks to his 24-hour bakery, I now had a place to seek refuge.

I pushed the door open. The store was warm from the heat of the freshly baked goods. He looked at me with his bright, brown eyes. He didn't have his chef's hat on. He was wearing his regular clothes, not his usual white baker's uniform. Was the bakery closed for the day? Hurried and desperate, the words rushed out all at once.

'Hide me,' I said without a hint of a stutter. They would never look for me in a bakery just a few hundred metres from the apartment complex.

He didn't ask questions, or speak, or nod. He simply opened the door to the kitchen where the sweet smell of chocolate still hung in the air. He said nothing, but his wide shoulders seemed to usher me in.

The kitchen had the look of an ordinary bakery kitchen, not that I knew much about commercial kitchens. Inside were two enormous ovens. He opened the door to the slightly larger oven, pulled out the racks, and looked at me. Did he want me to hide in there? In that moment, I thought of the witch that was burned alive – the one who bided her time fattening Hansel up, but fell head first into the woodstove thanks to Gretel's cunning. Was I the witch or Gretel in that story?

But there was no time to think. I put one foot in the still-warm oven, wondering why he wasn't telling me to take off my shoes first. Was this sanitary?

As he gestured with his chin to get in, I stammered, 'Okay, b–but don't t–turn on the oven.'

Chapter 1

The Hazel Branch

It all began with Mrs Bae and her eight-year-old daughter.

For the sake of convenience, I will refer to her as 'Mrs Bae' from here on, though I did call her 'Mother' for some time out of respect for her position as my father's wife. But the term hardly makes sense now that our lives fit together about as comfortably as joints out of sockets. Her last name is Bae and she's a primary schoolteacher by profession, so 'Mrs Bae' will suffice.

When Mrs Bae first came to our house, I was ten – the perfect age to start telling reality from fairy tale. When we are little, our underdeveloped intelligence makes it difficult for us to distinguish reality from fiction. But past a certain age, the human mind finds itself in a state of confusion brought on by the clash between expectation and reality. The majority gives up the fairy tale after a brief indulgence in the fantasy,

and a small minority either hangs itself or goes insane.
I was one of the majority.

Or maybe not. I lost my faith in fairy tales at six, in
the sea of people at Cheongnyangni Station where I
stuck my hands in my coat pockets and found my reality: four 500-won coins, a piece of pastry wrapped in
plastic packaging, and a crappy travel-size pack of tissues bearing the name of some karaoke bar.

Father thought an extravagant ceremony would be
too much for a second wedding and suggested they
just merge households and start living together. Mrs
Bae would not hear of it. She argued that she was neither some charity case fleeing from a bad marriage nor
a slave being dragged into this one. She didn't want to
just sign a piece of paper and start being his housewife.
She wanted a grand wedding with soap bubbles and
dry ice. A wedding where I would be present, not just
as a guest, but as the ring-bearer.

That was probably her way of declaring, *I am not a
maid your father has hired to cook your meals and do your
laundry. I am your father's wife. Be advised that I am in the
position to wield maternal power over you in every way.*

Her attempt to send this not-so-subtle message reflects
Mrs Bae's anxiety. Did she expect me to announce that
I couldn't accept her as a mother, the way kids do on
TV shows? Refuse to go to school, throw sand in my
rice, and make trouble in any of these typically juvenile
ways? Was she trying to establish her dominance from

the start so there wouldn't be any confusion about who's boss?

If so, she'd misjudged me by a mile. I had never mourned my mother's absence or felt the sort of bond with my father that would compel me to stake a claim over anyone. One can't be territorial about things they never had to begin with, or things that were taken away from them very early.

Anyway, thus began my cohabitation with Mrs Bae.

Before Father set the date, he summoned me for a confounding, cringy speech: 'You probably want to believe what they say in fairy tales because you're still a boy, but I think you know by now that those stories are all lies, don't you? There aren't any stepmothers in this world who behave like Cinderella's or Snow White's stepmothers.' (Father didn't know that in alternate versions of Snow White, the witch is actually Snow White's birth mother.) 'You had a bad experience with your mother, so I suppose you understand what I'm saying. Your stepmother-to-be is someone who will keep her promise to the end. She won't be nice to you today and mean tomorrow. And she's a schoolteacher, too. She understands children very well. She will never treat you unfairly or be out of line with you. She's a good person, so be sure to listen to her and call her "Mum".'

Father wanted fresh underwear and pressed shirts to

appear in his dresser every day. He wanted to wake up to the smell of delicious soup and beansprouts tossed in sesame sauce tickling his nose. In summary, that was why he was getting married again.

Father was so antsy that I wouldn't get along with Mrs Bae. He must have pictured me building my own little shrine for my mother in the backyard and shaking the hazel branch that bears my mother's spirit, cursing Mrs Bae's name. (The fabled hazel branch probably doesn't manifest its amazing power unless the deceased mother loved her child dearly and wished for her child's happiness with all her heart.) I picked up this browbeating message in Father's careful consolation and gestures of coercion: *What could you possibly do at this point when things have progressed this far, throw a tantrum? Give up, okay?*

Merely promising I wouldn't cause trouble wasn't enough for Father; he demanded enthusiastic and wholehearted support for this marriage. He persistently prodded me for the reaction he wanted. Expected submission.

Father said definitively that fairy-tale stepmothers absolutely do not exist in real life. I doubt there's any word in this world as oppressive as 'absolutely'. Fairy tales may be fiction, but they aren't complete nonsense either. Times and civilisations may come and go, but human nature does not change dramatically.

At first, Mrs Bae came bearing gifts, like a Play-Station, to earn my affection. The first time I saw her, she showed up hand-in-hand with her two-year-old daughter. The girl was a toddler who was just starting to run. Just as our eyes were about to meet, Mrs Bae wrapped her arm around the child's shoulders and drew her close to her side. The daughter looked up at me and rolled in her shoulders, a gesture of fear.

I couldn't tell which was the case: did Mrs Bae see that the girl was frightened of me and hold her close to comfort her, or had the girl become frightened of me as a reaction to Mrs Bae's protective gesture? Which-ever the case, this created a learned rather than innate distance between the girl and me. It all happened in the blink of an eye and was over before I could com-prehend it. I might have been distracted by the PlayStation Mrs Bae handed me just then.

The best plan of action for domestic peace would have been to stay within our boundaries. Show only an appropriate amount of interest, participate in the dozen or so family functions – birthdays of older family members, memorial days, holidays – with as little friction as possible, and act the part of good, responsible family members.

For me, this was role play with an expiration date. Simply put, I figured time would pass and a dynamic would soon form whether or not I did anything about it, and so there was no need for me to particularly endear myself to her or keep her at arm's length.

I don't know if I ultimately did not warm to her because of her early attempts to establish dominance around the house or she was hurt by my lack of interest in her and turned against me, but I was not old enough to detect and cater to others' unvoiced emotional needs.

The plan would work as long as we did not take more than our share. I was guaranteed clothes, food and shelter, the basic foundation of a childhood, while Mrs Bae could receive social acceptance and legal protection for her daughter and herself by getting a husband. Maintaining tension between us, not too taut or too loose, we were able to remain a 'we' within that structure woven by those conditions. At least until the day of that incident with Muhee.

A few years after the PlayStation, Mrs Bae stopped trying to hide her contempt for me. I could guess where she was coming from. Except for fires and traffic accidents leading to PTSD, emotional distress is usually caused by a combination of factors that cannot be narrowed down to just one. But if I had to identify a major cause, I would say it was Father's fault.

Father was patriarchy incarnate, not exactly an

affectionate man to anyone in the family, including me. He thought that it was the woman's job to take care of all domestic matters. The business manager of a relatively prominent toy company, he might have been friendly to his customers – children and their parents – but at home, he was nothing like the colourful, charming toys he sold. He contributed to the family economy by going to work early and staying at the office late, and did nothing else. He had no hobbies or interests. Socially, he was in favour of gender segregation. Politically, he was a fan of right-wing nutjobs. But I never attempted to discuss politics to confirm his views, knowing how that would have gone down.

But it's impossible to avoid a parent you live with, at all times. The odd report card or school fee slips necessitated an occasional early-morning or late-night chat with my father. I made fastidious preparations to get us swiftly and casually through these meetings, but I seemed to bring out comments in him that led to trouble. Sometimes, he would say something like the following, no subtext intended: 'Your mum did well in school. You need to shape up.'

Each time he made a reference to my dead mother, I would find Mrs Bae over Father's shoulder. In the way she silently stared down at the back of his head, I could hear her frigid voice ringing, *What are you saying? Who do you mean by 'your mum'? What does that make me? Why do you insist on reminding me that this boy had another mother?*

Little things that happy, sunny people might let slide bothered her.

'Why is this album on this shelf? Did you leave it out here for me to see?'

(If I had to map the coordinates of said album on the shelf, I would say it was x=100 and y=0. The album had not been moved in a hundred years.)

'Why are you asking me? Ask Father.'

'You left it lying around here for me to see! Don't you lie to me.'

'But I didn't.'

Why is she picking on me for no reason? I got up to leave, thinking that nothing good would come of being around her for longer than necessary (and that is how I came to spend long hours confined to my room).

'Why is this album with old family photos out in the open for me to see?'

'Like I said, you should ask Father.'

'Aren't you a part of this family? Your father isn't here right now to answer my question! Are you implying that this is none of my business?'

'Um . . . that's not what I'm saying . . .'

'Who else besides you here is supposed to know what your father's up to? Don't give me that look. You think I don't have the right to ask these questions, do you? Or that I don't deserve an explanation? Well, I suppose that means there's no reason for you to grace me with your presence. Go to your room.'

These little episodes piled up and closed in on my territory in the house.

I would sometimes turn on the CD player in the living room for music homework, and she would come in ten minutes later to unplug the stereo and walk away. Before I could ask why she had done that, she would retreat from the room saying, 'I have such a headache!'

Once, when I was working on a school project in the living room while watching TV, she came into the room and saw the scissors, glue, wooden sticks and paper strewn about on the living-room table. She picked everything up by the tablecloth, and moved it into my room.

'I don't tolerate mess in my house. I hope you understand.'

I suppose she still had the decency to ask for my understanding at the time.

These incidents kept piling up one on top of the other until, by the end of Year 6, greeting her when I returned from school became the most unbearable moment of my day. I bowed as deeply as possible to avoid eye contact with her, and lifted my head only after her slippers had silently disappeared from my peripheral vision.

Mrs Bae wanted her second marriage to be everything her first was not, but Father didn't live up to her expectations. No surprises there. He married only for the perks of the arrangement. After all, he had paid an arm and a leg to the matchmaking industry to find a woman of some social standing who would keep the house in order and take care of his mother who lived by herself.

But just because I sympathised with her personal anguish it didn't mean it fell on me, the son of the ex-wife, to help her through another bad marriage. I had just enough patience and energy to put up with Father. My plan was to disappear the instant I had the means to manage on my own, and I hoped she would do me the kindness of tolerating me until the day came. Think of me as no more than a thick plume of air that would blow away soon enough and stop trying to fit me into her idea of a picture-perfect family.

Consider this scene: a holiday gathering of thirty or so relatives. Among the cousins I saw a few times every year were people like Father's cousin who missed a few gatherings to tend to other extended family. I was seeing him for the first time in years.

'Who have we here?' the cousin said, giving me a slap on the shoulder. 'It's you, the little genius! Remember how we used to call him a genius when he was young? He started reading when he was two, and wrote

picture diaries at four when most kids don't even have
the motor skills to hold a pencil! He was a sensation
around here! Remember?' (Relatives one hardly ever
sees never know what to say besides recount stories
from your baby days.)

The adults all roared with laughter and said everyone thinks their child's a genius when they're little.
*So-and-so memorised the multiplication table at three, but
he's not even in the ninetieth percentile at his school now. My
eldest memorised the flags and capitals of all the countries
when she was two, but now* . . . and then they asked Mrs
Bae for her opinion as the educator.

'Well,' said she, 'I don't think it matters what kids do
when they're young. Even if it does make a difference
in nurturing their talents, I will never put Muhee
through "gifted programmes". Considering our educational system, such programmes might do more harm
than good. The programmes might lead the child to
delinquency, and the kids who participate in the programmes are used for commercial gain and then
abandoned. I don't care how phenomenal the kid is –
you just never can tell how they're going to turn out. So
I am not for it. It's not for Muhee.'

Mrs Bae's speech was quickly forgotten in the ensu-
ing sound of glasses being refilled. But the fact that she
stressed twice that she wouldn't let Muhee get that
way, that she never once looked at me but chose to
stare into the eye of the grilled fish on the table for

that speech, and that it wasn't clear who this 'phenomenal' kid she was referring to was (me, or gifted
kids in general?), told me that the comment hit a
nerve. Considering I was a perfectly average student
who never distinguished himself in any way apart
from small prizes for school writing contests, Mrs Bae
only served to expose her insecurity by bringing up
gifted programmes, *which no one asked about.*

Actually, I think the oblivious, insensitive relative's
semi-audible comment, 'He's such a good writer. He
gets that from his mother,' was what set Mrs Bae off.
That relative, of course, knew nothing about what
happened between Mum and me.

Just as Mrs Bae's passive-aggressive gestures and
comments built up over time and stifled me, I imagine
she was frustrated and exhausted by her need for vali-
dation. The incidents carried little meaning on their
own, but they collected like atoms and turned into
something with substance.

But it wasn't my fault, unless existing is a crime.

Mrs Bae's demands, though the delivery left much to
be desired, were small and often quite reasonable
enough that I did not notice until they turned into an
unreasonable burden.

'You're old enough. When are you going to start
doing your own laundry? You don't know how to

operate a washing machine? What a fine job your
father did raising you! Come watch and learn. Do
your own wash. It's not like I'm telling you to go beat
your clothes against a rock with a club – the machine
does everything. Why do I have to do this for you? It's
just washing, hanging and drying.'

'Now that I've fed you dinner, why don't you make
yourself useful and do the dishes? Do I have to show
you how? I'm not your maid.'

'Iron your own shirts. You're in secondary school
now – you're old enough. You have nothing else to
wear, anyway, now that you're wearing school uniform. It's not like I'm telling you to iron all the shirts
in this house.'

I figured if this was her way of calling attention to
the imbalance in household chore distribution, I
would do it for domestic peace. So I complied right
away. But I sensed that there were other underlying
problems that her myopic, superficial solutions could
not fix.

I began to fear for my life . . . or maybe just feel my
space in the house close in, when Mrs Bae started to
criticise the way I dressed at home.

'Don't think that you own this place. "It's the
summer and it's hot?" Turn on the fan. Going around
half-naked isn't going to help. Can't you stop wandering around the house in your shorts and tanks? I can't

imagine who raised you to be so crass. Don't you have T-shirts? And why are you wandering around the house barefoot when we have slippers? I don't care what you do in your room, but don't do that in the common area. This isn't just your house – it's mine, too. Mind your manners.'

Mrs Bae's desire for space gradually manifested itself more explicitly. It was the sort of desire that intensifies with the feeling that the people you live with aren't on your side, and that the place you live in is not your home. Mrs Bae's every frustrated, ugly gesture screamed, *This is my house. I am in charge here!* Behind the scream was Muhee's sullen face. Was that what she was worried about? That I would invade her space and take what belonged to my little stepsister?

Once I concluded this might be the case, I started sticking to a certain routine. I got into the habit of leaving the house at the crack of dawn and getting bread at the school shop for breakfast. It was my way of keeping to a minimum the time I spent in Mrs Bae's space and put myself at her mercy. I picked up a snack at the bakery on the way home to eat in my room. I would slip into my room, which was right by the front door, and close the door behind me. That was the space I was granted. That door did not open again until the next day, when I woke up early to use the bathroom before anyone else, except under unfortunate circumstances such as diarrhoea, high fever, or an inflamed appendix. I did my homework on the word processor and listened to the sound of the struggling laser printer mingle with the dialogue from the TV soap playing in the living room.

Father, who usually came home around midnight, had no way of knowing this. I turned the lights out right before midnight and crawled under the covers. I closed my eyes and listened to the front door unbolt, followed by Father's disgruntled, 'That son of mine doesn't bother to poke his head out when his father comes home. Always sleeping like a lazy bum.'

Father, don't you know that your wife doesn't like standing next to me to greet you when you come home? Don't you know that when her hand accidentally grazes mine during one of those rare occasions when the 'family' gathers to have a meal together, she recoils as though she's been stung? Don't you know that I spend the rare yet painfully awkward family meals with my eyes fixed on the tablecloth to avoid trouble?

Not long after I entered secondary school, I made the problem student list.

'That kid – he apparently turned that way towards the end of primary school.'

'Hmmph. I think he's doing it for the attention. He can read out loud just fine.'

'The thing is, he gets that way when he doesn't have

the words in front of him. I feel uncomfortable calling on him in class. His grades are average, and there's nothing off about him besides the speech thing.'

'He doesn't hang out with anybody.'

'Well, it doesn't matter if he hangs out with anybody. Just make sure he's not completely isolated and bullied. I don't think he requires much care beyond that.'

The information spread through the grapevine and made it into my school record, labelling me a moderately unfortunate kid. Therapy was recommended.

While the whispering continued, a Korean lit teacher who happened to be in charge of the school pastoral care centre kindly set up a session and stayed behind after school. She kept telling me to open up. She said that I would overcome my problems if I found their roots. But who could I safely open up to? What would I say? That I know a really competent teacher like you people, who happens to be my father's wife, who turns everything into an issue and picks fights just because I'm her new husband's son? That she needs therapy, not me? This was just the kind of thing that would come back to haunt me several degrees of separation later.

Knowing the reason was not going to change the situation, so the less said about it, the better. So I spoke less and less until I lost my words.

After the unproductive session, I felt tired as if I'd

just gone running at full speed. I came back to the classroom and loosened my tie. What kind of old-fashioned secondary-school kid goes to the school pastoral care centre for help these days? That was like digging a hole in the ground and whispering, 'King Midas has donkey ears.' Online forums was the place to get decent advice, or at least some sympathetic responses.

'Is your mouth just for show? Tell your father! Tell him that she's harassing and abusing you. Why can't you just say it?'

'Look, you stupid little twerp. You don't know what the hell you're talking about. You don't know anything about the consequences of ratting like that, so STFU.'

'I'm kinda going through the opposite case, because I ratted everything to my mum. She wouldn't believe me or my step-father even after I showed her what he did to my forehead. Do you know how much it just makes you want to blow your brains out when something like that happens? I wanted to rip out the ten stitches that the bastard paid for. You have no fucking idea what that feels like.'

So there were conflicting views. But the consensus of the middle-class kids was to think practically.

'Try not to think about it. Just suck it up and take it for a few years, then you can move into a college dorm or get a job and move out. Who's going to stop you then? If you run away now, you'll have nowhere to go. There's nothing you can do out there without money.'

So, two more years of this?

What made me afraid and uncomfortable was that instead of holding my head underwater in the bathtub, Mrs Bae was cleverly sucking the life out of me with her cost-efficient schoolteacher approach. Minimum effort, maximum trauma. Psychological injury without a single violet bruise on the skin.

When people come across Cinderella characters in movies who suffer silently and let the abuse continue, they say, 'What the hell is wrong with that moron? Why live like that? Just tell on the stepmother and get the hell out of there!' But even as people say this, they know very well that those who expose injustice often suffer more injustice, that one cannot survive without financial support, and that certain forms of abuse one has no choice but to endure to achieve one's goals.

If I didn't have to suffer the consequences of speaking out, there would have been the chasm between reality and the ideal, I would have had to contend with out on my own: the assumption that kids who prepare their futures at a youth shelter are ones who ran from life-threatening violence or a poor family they couldn't get anything out of even if they stuck it out; or the middle-class faith that college will solve some if not all of your problems.

In the end, I chose the path most travelled. And to take that path, the more material resources I had, the better. I would not give Mrs Bae the satisfaction of going off the path I was expected to take. I determined the course of action with my long-term plan in mind, making calculations in preparation for my to-be-determined date of departure.

But then, I must have pressed the wrong button somewhere because my life began to go wildly off course.

It was a crimson bloodstain.

I was about to do laundry when I saw a pair of Muhee's pants in my hamper. The speckled trace of blood reminded me of magnolia petals in the late spring, fallen and trampled upon. The hamper slipped out of my hands and my clothes scattered on the laundry-room floor. Just then, I saw Mrs Bae who had come out into the kitchen to make dinner. She stared me up and down trying to figure out what was going on and then snatched her daughter's underwear off the floor.

That night, I lay in my room in the dark trying not to listen, pretending I didn't know, but the voices kept intruding through the earbuds blasting music in my ear. She was grilling the little girl. Did it happen at school? Or the English academy? Is it someone your age? A little older? A grown-up? Muhee was overwhelmed by all the questions being thrown at her. She had trouble making sense. Father stepped in: 'She can't talk with you driving her crazy like this. Calm down and listen to her . . .' 'You, stay out of this!' A few barks and slaps, and the affair soon turned into a fight between the adults.

I suppose Mrs Bae dragged out the basic details in the midst of that chaos. The next day, she received a doctor's note that her injuries would take four weeks to heal, and barged into Muhee's after-school English academy.

After being tortured by her mother's persistent interrogation, Muhee had finally identified the Conversational English teacher, who, coincidentally, had a history of some similar charge. It wasn't clear if it was a misunderstanding, or if he did time, or if the affair was swept under the rug with a settlement, but he'd had to leave his previous job because of it.

A thorough investigation of the teacher revealed that the biography printed on the English academy ad when the academy first opened was all made up. The ad said that he lived abroad for about fifteen years since childhood, finished secondary school there and received his university degree in Korea. That was how he was able to work at the academy where the director almost exclusively hired native speakers. However, it turned out he only lived abroad for around two years, was a university dropout, and nothing else on his CV was true other than the fact that he did, in fact, speak English fluently.

The academy director, concerned about unpleasant rumours affecting business, offered Mrs Bae 10 million won to keep quiet.

'Could you be discreet about this? We weren't aware of this when we hired him, either. If there's a problem, you should come to us instead of walking into the classroom and attacking the teacher in the middle of class. We don't know exactly what happened at this point, and word will spread online. What if enrolment goes down? Look. No one else has come forward with charges against him. Don't you think that's strange? How do you know your kid isn't naming him when it was really someone else?'

'Are you calling my daughter a liar?'

Muhee was attacked and accused of lying about it, and Mrs Bae would not stand for it. She took the medical diagnosis and the pen recorder containing her phone conversation with the academy director to the prosecutor's office. This was after she had another big fight with Father who said that if she made too big a deal out of this, Muhee would remember this for ever and be scarred for life.

A week later, the mother and daughter began their series of interrogations at the prosecutor's office, where they were treated like offenders.

'An awful thing has happened to an eight-year-old girl and the son of a bitch prosecutor kept asking her all these terrible questions like "Muhee, can you point

to where the teacher touched you? Did he put anything else in there besides his hand? A pen, a chopstick?
What about his weenie? Did he make you look at it or
touch it? Did he make you put it in your mouth? How
big was it? This big, or that big?" I couldn't stand it
any more and said, "What the hell does it matter how
big it was?" And he said they had to make sure it was
an adult, not a child. He said that he'd make me leave
the room if I interrupted him again. I am her mother!
How can you ask such degrading questions in front of
the child's mother!'

Quiet sympathy was the least Father could offer, but
he chose instead to say, 'I told you so. It was your idea
to drag the poor girl through this, knowing damn
well what you were signing up for. Just drop it and
settle the matter by moving her to a different English
academy. And don't even think about taking that
insulting settlement.'

'Okay, so I agree with you about the settlement, but
how dare you tell me to drop it? Would you say that if
she were your daughter? Well, lucky you – you only
have a son!'

'How can you say that? He's your son, too.'

'You're the one who's always thinking of them in
terms of yours or mine, so what the hell do you want
from me? If we're not in this together, fine. We don't
need you. I'm going to fight to the bitter end. I'm

going to destroy them all – the academy, that bastard, everything!'

I didn't care about any of this, but I had nothing against Muhee and was therefore not delighting in Mrs Bae's predicament. In any case, I figured she'd want me to stay out of this, as with everything. I tried not to breathe a word about it. This, however, provoked her.

'You couldn't care less what's going on under this roof! Life must be a bowl of cherries for you. And your father! Would you be so insensitive if I were your mother? If Muhee were your little sister?'

But my expression of interest in the matter or gestures of concern also annoyed Mrs Bae.

'What do you know? Can't you see the adults are talking? Where are your manners?'

Damned if I do, damned if I don't.

Because Muhee consistently identified the English teacher as the culprit, the prosecutor's office arranged a three-party interview. The teacher in question was apparently very calm and collected.

'I completely understand how a mother would feel if her daughter's gone through something like that. I have children, too. But you're making a mistake, ma'am. I'm not going to ask how or where you found out about my past, but the source of that information doesn't appear legitimate or legal. As someone who raises and teaches children, I sympathise with you. Regarding that incident in the past, all parties involved agreed that it was a misunderstanding and apologised. And what about this case? If several kids made the same claims, I really would deserve no less than death. But that's not the case. Thanks to you, I'm going to get fired from my job, and all things considered, the damage I've suffered is much greater than yours. But whether I like it or not, I've been through this before, so I'm going to think of this as just bad luck. If you drop this now, I won't press charges against you for ruining an innocent person's reputation. I'm quitting soon, and I don't want to cause the academy any more trouble.'

'Innocent? Are you conspiring with the academy to turn my daughter into a liar?'

'Hey, lady! Take it easy!' the prosecutor interjected. 'Lower your voice! Where do you think you are? And fella, keep your answers short. Do you know why you're here? You're here so the kid can identify you one more time.'

The fact that the prosecutor called her 'lady' every single time and dropped the honorific for teachers, despite the fact that he knew she was a teacher, got on her nerves. All prosecutors are a little different, but Mrs Bae's theory was that the majority of them often omitted honorifics to intimidate offenders and victims alike.

'Who are you calling "lady"? Maybe I should call

you "buddy"! Hey, buddy, you ever raise kids? If your kid was raped, would you be trying so hard to prove that your kid's a liar?'

'I'm not married,' said the prosecutor.

'Surprise, surprise.'

'Going back to our main business here, I never said the girl was lying. I'm just saying you shouldn't pin the crime on someone before thinking long and hard about it. Things will get pretty hairy if you end up ruining someone who didn't do anything. You too, kid. I want you to think very hard about this before you answer! If it later turns out that you were lying, you or your mum will go to jail!'

'What kind of a prosecutor threatens a child! I'm going to post this on the internet!'

'Ooh, the internet! You think the internet is the answer to everything? Go ahead, post away!'

And so the tables turned and turned again. Muhee consistently identified the English teacher as the offender three or four times in a row, but at around the seventh time the prosecutor asked her, she put Mrs Bae in an awkward position by saying she couldn't remember, not paying attention, or bursting into tears.

'Look. The current legal system in Korea requires physical evidence to prosecute someone. It's realistically difficult to take a child's testimony as evidence. They say that the very first testimony made in a calm environment in the presence of a child psychologist should count as evidence, but that works only in theory. They should try applying that in the field themselves. That's right. You're a teacher, aren't you? So you know how often children lie without realising it. It's not that they are being malicious, is it? Children are like ostriches with their heads in the sand . . . 75 per cent of all child sex offenders are someone the child knows. Of the 75 per cent, 38 are someone from the neighbourhood, 19 are relatives, 17 are from educational institutions . . . So stop picking on one person and cast the net wide.'

And then, one night, everything came to a head.

Mrs Bae had received a subpoena that day. The English teacher had a change of heart when Muhee changed her testimony, and pressed charges against the English academy and Mrs Bae for defamation. Mrs Bae grabbed Muhee by the hair that night and whipped her with a wire coat hanger as the girl begged for her life.

'Say it! Say it! Who did it? If it wasn't that bastard, who was it? You bitch, you made me look like an idiot by going after the wrong person and now I've fucking lost face! You don't deserve to live! Spit it out! Which asshole was it? Tell the truth!'

Mrs Bae was beating her in front of me as though she wanted me to play audience. I had nothing against Muhee, but I didn't feel chivalrous enough to step in and shield her either, so I didn't try to stop Mrs Bae. I had learned from experience that if I butted in, she would shove me aside with some minor insult and hit Muhee even harder.

And then it happened.

I stood there, my mind drawing a blank as I tried to understand the meaning of Muhee's hand rising slowly, a lone finger pointing at my face.

Mrs Bae's dry palm flew at me in slow motion and scratched my cheekbone. I hit the back of my head hard as she seized me by the collar and slammed me against the wall. Only then did I understand what was happening to me. I heard a vein pop on impact, sending a tingling, warm sensation through my head.

It's not true! No! Why would I do such a thing? I have no way of knowing if these cries and protests actually came out of me. The shower of punches and slaps that followed immediately left me in a daze. I wasn't small or weak. I now reached Father's shoulder, had the strength to stand up against her blows, and could have returned the attack and then some, but I didn't. Father was watching. I couldn't do that to Father's wife. I wound up kneeling with my head bowed to the floor. Her slippered foot came down over my neck and my back.

Feeling a warm stream of liquid flowing from the corner of my mouth down to the chin, I raised my head to look at Father. The look on his face suggested that he didn't really believe Muhee, but didn't care enough, either, to defend me. Overall, his expression was inscrutable.

You know it wasn't me, right? You believe I wouldn't do such a thing, right? I don't know if these thoughts were voiced out loud, or if they just echoed in my head. What was clear, however, was that the flushed Mrs Bae finally stopped kicking to push past Father and pick up the phone.

'Hello? Police? I would like to report a juvenile criminal.'

At that moment, something snapped inside me. It was no time for childish beliefs that I would be proved innocent because the accusation was untrue and there was no evidence. Father didn't stop Mrs Bae from picking up the phone, so how could I expect a fairy-tale ending of forgiveness and reconciliation in this house? Of the restoration of everyday peace? We were caught in a storm, and I was the prisoner of war or foreigner they were throwing overboard to keep the vessel from sinking.

The moment this occurred to me, I shoved Mrs Bae, who had got off the phone and resumed strangling me. She fell over and knocked Father over as well. Leaving the two to struggle like a pair of overturned turtles, I opened the front door.

Before I dashed out of there, I briefly made eye contact with Muhee, who was standing by the bedroom door, her nose still bleeding. I didn't have time to dawdle, but I was able to give her a slight nod that said, *It's not your fault.* I didn't have to ask to know that she had to point at someone to save herself, and that someone just happened to be me.

I heard Mrs Bae screaming behind me, 'Stop him!' and Father shuffling to pick himself up. They were coming after me.

Chapter 2

The Devil's Cinnamon Cookies

The Devil's Cinnamon Cookies
2 per serving.
9,000 won.

Ingredients: flour, cinnamon, brown sugar, raisins and a secret extract. The contents of the extract will not be revealed, as some may find certain ingredients revolting. (Baker's note: Contents of the extract are generally not considered an allergen. Besides, you're not going to eat it yourself!)

Product Details: Feed this to someone you don't like. The cookie will leave the person's mental capacity in disarray for an average of two hours so that the person will fail in all endeavours. If the person is giving an important presentation or making a crucial statement, the subjects and predicates will not match. The person will ramble and appear idiotic to anyone present. If the person is full at the moment, they may lose control of their bowels. If consumed on an empty stomach, it induces continuous vomiting. Legends say that one infamous lawyer who snacked on this cookie before trial was thrown out of court and disbarred!

Directions: Keep the product wrapped in the brown oil-paper it came in. Please note that product potency wears off if stored in another container. At approximately 5 a.m. on the day of use, place this product westward before the sun comes up and say, 'With all my fury and hatred, I wish upon [insert enemy's name here] what they deserve.' (Note: All incantations that come with The Wizard's Bakery products are original Latin or Ancient Greek spells translated and made user-friendly. The potency of the spell, therefore, may be weaker, so please do not take the recitation lightly. Say it from your heart and be sure to enunciate.)

The web address of the wizard baker's online shop was wizardsbakery.com. This website sold various mystical and questionable products. Given the nature of these products, I imagined the store would be small-scale and underground like those internet message board businesses, but many people ordered things here, posted on message boards and left product ratings on the review page. Although some of the products were on the pricey side, there was no credit card payment system, just an offshore account customers could wire payments to. If they received credit card payments, the transactions would be traceable. The store would be shut down instantly and the wizard would be arrested for selling 'love potions' and 'voodoo dolls' that actually worked.

There were plenty of strange, politically incorrect products people sold and bought on auction sites, the ads for which read, 'Use my forehead as a billboard', 'Adopt the ghost that lives in our house for 1,000 won. Free shipping. You won't need A/C ever again', or 'Physically healthy, gets excellent grades, cultured. Seeking someone to buy me.' However, the products sold at the wizard's online shop were inherently different from these sketchy, ridiculous things.

In exchange for hiding out at the shop, I was asked to manage the shop's website.

'By "managing" the website, I don't mean anything fancy. Just check the website regularly and let me know when something comes up on the message board or if there's an order. You won't be able to answer any questions regarding products unless they're about payment and shipping, but let me know right away when an order comes in. It's a bit of a hassle, but that way I can work on the orders throughout the day. I've been making them all at once at night so far.'

So. What did the baker sell on his website?

First of all, there were the mysterious pastries. They didn't look very different from the ones sold at regular bakeries, but the ingredients were a little unusual. The ones sold in the shop did not contain any of the ingredients he named that day when I asked him what was in them, of course. The pastry that looked identical to the ones at the store but contained the foul or freaky ingredients were carefully wrapped and shipped off to various people who ordered them online.

And who were these people ordering these 'treats'?

Each product had a detailed image, a partial list of ingredients and the effect on the person who consumed it. At the bottom of the product details was a thorough list of the side effects. After the product details section was a review section where people rated the products and posted comments. There were stories of people who bought it just for fun and were pleasantly surprised by the results, whether or not they believed the product truly did have magical properties. The star ratings for the products were generally three and a half to four out of five stars. The effects ranged from gaining the confidence and composure to close an important business deal ('I don't care if it was a placebo effect, as long as the outcome was good!') or someone's evil boss messing up the presentation on a new product, to reciprocated affection.

The Devil's Cinnamon Cookies were one of around twenty kinds of pastries and cookies on the website. The product had a wide range of effects – positive, negative, neutral. These are a few I found interesting:

Willpower Custard Pudding – Top Seller!

An edible talisman against bad luck and the yips for exam periods or important business trips.

Peacemaking Raisin Scone

Give it to someone as an apology. Your apology will be accepted, 100% guaranteed. Product may not work if you are apologising without genuine remorse.

Broken-hearted Pineapple Madeleine – Top Seller!

Helps your broken heart heal faster. As its baker, though, I would not recommend it. You may end up in a meaningless rebound fling in your hasty rush to get over the relationship.

'No, Thank You' Sablé Chocolat

Trying to spurn someone's advances? Give them this in lieu of an answer. They will eat this instead of eating their heart out.

Business Egg Muffins

A nice gift basket for people who are starting a new business. It may not bring them monumental success or wealth, but they will stay in business for a long time. At the very least, they won't go under. Doesn't work for greedy people who keep expanding the business beyond their means.

Amaretto Memory Stick – Top Seller!
Eat this and meditate. You will be revisited by a very vivid memory that you've lost or you least want to remember. What's in your subconscious? What memories are you repressing? For the adventurous and curious.

Forget-Me-Not Mocha Manju
Give it to a friend who is going away – transferring, going abroad to study, emigrating, etc. Your friend will never forget you. Your friend will think of you every time he or she is sad or happy, and won't be able to resist looking you up.

Doppelgänger Financier
Depending on the spell, if you eat this before you go to sleep at night, your doppelgänger will go to school or work in your place. Kick back and relax at home, or play hooky somewhere. Please note that you must never show up at school or work to find out if your doppelgänger really did show up for you. If people see the two of you together or if you make eye contact with your doppelgänger, one of you will disappear for ever – guess which one.

On the last line of each product detail was an interesting warning:

'The changes that take place as a consequence of your wish, whether positive or negative, affect the order of the physical and metaphysical world. Therefore, do remember that when using the power of magic, this energy has the potential to come back and return the favour.'

Was he trying to discourage people from buying these products? There was also something similar in the Terms of Agreement on the webpage, which read, 'All magic spells are cast with the understanding that the effect may return to you. Please use products responsibly.'

On the bottom were the raised buttons, 'Yes, I accept.'/ 'No, I do not accept.'

In other words, if you planned to strangle some-body, you had to accept the possibility of one day being strangled yourself. I was thinking about using some of these products on Mrs Bae, but the thought quickly vanished. Nothing I wanted to do to her was worth the bad karma circling back to me.

Anyway, there were at least twenty orders of The Devil's Cinnamon Cookie every day. If I didn't know better, I would have laughed at the people who believed in magic and casting spells on people, but after seeing what was inside the wizard's oven, I could no longer be cynical.

The overwhelming majority of our clientele were women in their teens deeply interested in astrology and tarot. The next largest group were women in their twenties. But on the client list, there were also the occasional male clients from all age groups and people in their fifties, although those were probably identity theft cases or kids using their parents' cards.

Voodoo dolls or The Red Notebook of Doom (in which one could lay a curse on someone by writing his or her name) were widely sold online as novelty items, but the wizardsbakery.com products were in a completely different league from those mass-produced, just-for-fun items. Considering we live in a society where market value is everything, whether you're selling matter or soul, I suppose it's not that surprising that one could build a business with magic products.

I slowly familiarised myself with the twenty products divided into four categories, spending most of the day printing out orders as they came in and passing them to the baker who was an oven door away. He said it helped him prepare ingredients or dough in advance if he knew what kinds of pastry or confections he had to make, but he might have made up a task so I'd have something to do all day.

In between these tasks, I sometimes wondered if Father and Mrs Bae had stopped looking for me, not knowing I was hiding in a neighbourhood bakery that didn't look like much from the outside.

Back to that night when I crawled into the wizard's oven.

The oven led to a cavern of unending darkness. I could simply curl up instead of crawling forward and still be devoured by the darkness. I wandered on in, not knowing whether it was safe. I had no choice.

Was this a portal to another world like I once saw in a movie? Like Narnia beyond a closet, with its thick, magnificent, virgin forest, white snow no one in the world has ever trodden upon, talking animals, centaurs, vines that have a mind of their own, people made of sand?

I heard him close the door behind me with an unfeeling clank. I closed my eyes and felt my way forward. Instead of an empty space of boundless depth, I felt something hard like a glass surface on my hands. I pushed it and saw another space open up before my eyes.

Where was I?

I found myself in a studio about twenty times larger than the bakery. A room of these dimensions couldn't possibly exist in a building this size. I stepped down onto the floor, and heard another door shut behind me with a clank. I turned around to see another oven. Is that what I'd just crawled out of? I carefully opened the oven door. I reached in as far as I could. I couldn't feel anything in there, as expected, except a primordial, boundless darkness.

The studio was quite spacious. The large burgundy lab table in the middle of the room caught my eye. The table was full of intricate lab equipment whose names I didn't know. Flasks and beakers containing unidentifiable liquids of charming colours sat bubbling evenly over burners, giving off the gentle scent

of peppermint. Was it okay to leave them unattended?
What if they exploded?

On the other side of the wall was a luxurious bed
like the one Scheherazade would have laid upon in
Arabian Nights, and a desktop computer with a 21-inch
LCD monitor in a quaint, polished antique design.
The left wall was completely hidden behind a heavy,
sturdy-looking, walnut-coloured built-in bookcase.
The shelves were mostly filled with old hardback
books. I couldn't identify the language most of them
were in, but there were also a few with English or
Korean titles.

On the ceiling, so high I wouldn't be able to reach
it if I tried jumping on the bed, there were a breath-
taking number of constellations embroidered onto the
black surface. How was it possible to produce such a
natural-looking astronomical dome with man-made
lighting installation? Even the tail of the comet whiz-
zing through the stars looked real.

A velvet armchair sat next to the fireplace on the
right-hand wall. The fireplace was electric, not the
wood-burning kind, but it did produce heat and pretty
strong flames that caressed and licked the large cast-
iron cauldron hanging by two hooks installed on the
side wall inside the hearth. The sight of a real cauldron, known as the witch's womb, where ingredients
are decomposed and fermented, reminded me that I
was truly in the house of a wizard. White smoke

billowed out of the cauldron and dispersed through the air. I peeked in the pot to see what was boiling in there, and was disappointed to find water.

But the cauldron corrected my previous judgement of the baker as merely a nutcase. I had never thought about what I would do if I were to meet some mystical or magical creature in real life, but instead of panicking or pinching myself, I felt strangely relaxed and optimistic. When so many people believe in invisible things like gods and souls, why wouldn't I believe in something so real as a wizard's cauldron bubbling right here before my eyes?

Once I accepted what I saw, I could guess what the large circular diagram on the floor with straight and curved lines must be. It was a magic circle. There was a small six-point star in a larger twelve-point star, and there was an inscription in the spaces created by the lines that appeared to be Hebrew and mathematical equations. The star, in turn, was in two large concentric circles.

A wooden eight-drawer cabinet stood in the corner next to the bookcase. It looked like a filing cabinet you'd find in office furniture catalogues. Each drawer held a label written in a language I didn't know.

In all stories, the protagonist is guided by an intense curiosity as to what is behind doors ominously closed, which compels him to turn the doorknob or pull the handle. The door looks locked at first, but the latch opens with surprising ease and another world opens up. Or there's something sinister inside. That was the general idea of these traps so common in fairy tales and folklore. Open the forbidden door, and you become the newest addition to the Bluebeard Collection.

My knowledge of this paradigm did not stop me from reaching for the drawer handle like a by-the-book fairy-tale fool. The second my hand touched the handle, the bird who was quietly perched on top of the cuckoo clock swooped down and slapped my hand with her wing.

'Ow!'

I recoiled and looked at the bluebird, nursing my hand. I thought it was an ornament on the cuckoo clock, but there it was, flapping in the air and staring down at me.

'D-don't open?'

The bluebird turned and flew up on the drawer instead of answering. It looked somehow familiar. It was orange around the stomach and blue around the shoulders, the same blue and orange as the shirt and apron the girl behind the counter wore. Even the blue patch on the bird's head looked like the blue ribbon she always wore in her hair.

So you're the girl.

Bluebird bowed its head as if to nod and flew back up to its spot on the cuckoo clock.

Before I had time to wonder what I was to do here

now, the oven door clicked open. The baker leaned in from behind the door.

'Hey, what are you doing standing there?'

'Uhh . . .'

I had to say something. Give him some explanation or excuse. But then I remembered that I was a regular at the bakery and he knew that I stuttered. I didn't need to get my throat and tongue muscles tensed up trying to talk. The person standing before me, whatever he was, was special. I had a feeling he'd understand a lot of things without my having to say a word. This thought restored a sense of relief in my hands and feet, which didn't happen very often.

'I see you were curious about what's in there?'

See? Didn't have to say a word. He untied his apron and hung it on a hook by the fireplace.

'You've cut your hand. I bet it was her. There's nothing special in there. It's all just herbs, leaves, mushrooms and dried natural ingredients. The third drawer, however, has animal fur organised by species, and the fourth drawer is chemically treated animal entrails, also organised by species. She probably stopped you to prevent you from passing out, so don't mind her.'

I nodded. As curious as I was, entrails weren't my cup of tea. I had no complaints now that I knew it wasn't some fateful door that I shouldn't open (but really must open to keep the plot moving).

He swivelled the purple velvet easy chair that was facing the fireplace, and said, 'Sit.'

Sit? Why? Well, okay. I probably looked like a constipated cat pacing nervously around his room, and that's bad manners. I forgot all about the things that happened to me only twenty minutes before, and sat in the chair he was pointing at.

Once I was settled in, he held out his hand and said, 'Hand.'

He said it like I was his dog and he was giving me a command – 'Shake.'

'Show me your hand. You're hurt.'

Oh, that. It's just a little scratch.

I extended the hand Bluebird's wing grazed. The sharp part down the middle of one of her feathers had broken my skin and drawn a little drop of blood.

The baker placed a piece of cotton on the back of my hand, chose the seventh test tube from the left among the row of test tubes, and droppered the contents. His touch was like warm water.

The potion seeped into the cotton wool and prickled my hand. When he removed the cotton wool, the stinging stopped and the cut was gone. I would have to learn not to be surprised by anything that happened here.

He took another piece of cotton wool and did the same on my busted lip. I'd forgotten about it, but I think Mrs Bae's wedding ring had clipped me.

'And now, we talk. The police were here.'

I carefully pressed my hands into the front of my shirt. The strangling sensation from Mrs Bae's attack still remained. I had to press it down or the dam I'd carefully built would come crashing down and pour forth a river I wouldn't be able to hold back.

'They wanted to know if I'd seen a boy of average height and in his late teens. Wasn't surprised. This place is the only one around that's open at this hour, so they dropped in, naturally. Today's not the first time the police have popped in for a questioning. They drop by to ask about bar brawls, hit-and-runs, etc. I actually see those cops pretty often. I thought it'd be more suspicious if I told them I didn't see anything, so I said I saw someone who kinda fits the description run down the street past the bus station. They didn't ask much else.'

'Th-thank you.'

'They won't be back. They looked like they couldn't care less. Well, it's late. Why don't you get some sleep? Or are you hungry?'

He gestured at the extravagant bed. I shook my head. The bedroom décor was a bit much for me, and as a fugitive seeking refuge at his place, I didn't dare take over the host's bed. I pointed at the floor by the magic circle, meaning I would be happy to sleep there.

At this, he grabbed me by both shoulders and declared, 'No! Children should be in bed at this hour!

And I work a lot at night, so if you're tossing and turning on the other side of the door, I can't get work done. I could put you to sleep with magic dust, but I'm giving you the option of falling asleep on your own. So do as I say.'

And then came the disheartening words: 'Sleep, have breakfast, and go home.'

There was no permanent shelter. I couldn't depend on a stranger for ever. I knew that. Even if people knew the truth about what happened, they wouldn't want to interfere in someone else's 'family matter'. What I accomplished by hiding here was merely delaying the inevitable.

The tension holding me together, powerful as the web of a spider, gave out. Strength drained from my arms and hands as well. A crack appeared down my heart. The crack split, and a muggy, unpleasant air slipped in, and the feelings I was holding back flowed out through my eyes. The image of Father looking away from me and standing with his hands behind his back swirled before my eyes, which turned into Mrs Bae shaking me by the collar, which turned into Muhee's eyes looking a little guilty.

Oh, man.

I bit my lip, but I couldn't stop the sobs from leaking out.

'Cry. It'll make you feel better.'

Already crying, thanks.

'Look, you can cry out loud. Don't cover your face with your arm. Lift your chin.'

I lifted my head, and he put a glass test tube under my chin. I blinked, puzzled. A tear rolled down my chin and plopped into the test tube.

'Wh-what are you d-doing?'

'Children's tears are very useful.'

Who're you calling a child?

I figured this was just a wizard being a wizard, but he was being too true to his profession. Wouldn't a tissue be more appropriate under these circumstances?

'Different tears – happy, sad, angry, sentimental, undeserved scorn – all contain different elements. I can make a pretty wide range of potions with them. Excuse me – chin up!'

He held my chin with two fingers and moved it left and right to collect my tears. He was as swift as a nurse taking someone's blood sample without permission. On the one hand, I had a feeling he was making fun of me, but I was also grateful that I was too baffled to cry any more.

His tear collection was almost complete when Bluebird fluttered over and landed on his shoulder. She nuzzled her head against the side of his face, as though she was saying something in his ear.

'She must like you. She's saying you look like you're down on your luck and that we should keep you.'

I remembered that the girl at the counter was much

kinder and more friendly to the customers than the baker.

'We can't do that,' he continued, stroking her head. 'It's every man for himself. Things will work out for him if he's lucky, or maybe things will get worse. I hid him temporarily only because he's a regular. If he hides now, he'll be running from trouble for the rest of his life.'

Bluebird nuzzled harder against the wizard's neck. I felt grateful for her efforts, but he was probably right. But that didn't mean I could immediately muster up the strength to go home and face Mrs Bae's cold gaze, Father and his shifty eyes, and the police uncomfortably stuck in the middle of a 'family matter'. I needed time, at least until the cops filed this case as a regular runaway, and Mrs Bae calmed down enough to let me defend myself. If not that, maybe just enough time for me to compose a long letter arguing my innocence. Trying to talk my way out of it would only land me in more trouble.

After conversing with the bird in some mysterious way, the wizard seemed to have reached a conclusion.

'Hmm. I see your point. You're saying that we should grant him some time to regroup so he can stand up for himself. I hate to be bothered with things like this, but if you feel that strongly about this, fine. But you are cooking his meals and assigning him tasks. As you know, babysitting is not my forte.'

Watching Bluebird nod, I agonised between my situation and my dignity. I quietly bristled at words like 'bothered' and 'babysitting', but he was right. I was too old to be in someone's constant care, but lacked the last bit of confidence necessary to stand on my own two feet. I was sixteen – the most frustrating age.

Perhaps we could arrange this so that it didn't turn into 'unconditional protection'? Was there anything I could do to help?

'You d–don't want to know what h–h–happened?'

'I don't need to ask.'

Ah, that's right. All wizards come with a crystal ball or a magic mirror. So why isn't there one of those in this room? Does he look in the water in the cauldron instead? He could probably see things happening far away by looking into the palm of his hand.

'So you already know eh–eh–everything?'

'Nope. I'm not a god or a psychic.'

His answer was a little disappointing. He plodded over to the lab table, the flask of tears in hand, and carefully put a stopper on it. Why wasn't he curious?

'When it comes to humans, I'm not even a little curious.'

If my assumption was correct, if he really was a being from before there were beings, or a being greater than average beings, he probably had lived for a very, very long time. That would explain why he generally wasn't interested in human affairs.

'Although I'm not curious,' he continued from over at the lab table, his back towards me, 'I did notice a few things. A boy just barged into my store panting, shoelaces undone and shirt buttons torn off – I can tell that he's probably having a rough night. Judging from the red swelling around his neck and the busted lip, he most likely got into a row with someone, and if the adversary were someone his age, he could have gone home, but he came here instead, which means there's a good chance it was one of his family members, or that he's not safe in his house. The absence of any scratch marks on the back of his hand or a single piece of dead skin or hair underneath his fingernails suggests he couldn't fight back, which either means the opponent was someone older he wouldn't dare fight against, or that he's no good at hand-to-hand combat. The fact that a boy of his age and metabolism picks up bread at our store every evening suggests he doesn't eat dinner at home, which means he is either on bad terms with the person who prepares meals, or that there is no one to prepare meals for him. Conclusion: trouble at home. I think that about covers it, yes?'

In the few, brief moments he saw me from behind the counter of the bakery, he'd deduced this much about me. My jaw dropped. Perhaps it wasn't too late for a career change from baker to detective.

'Anyone can tell that much. But then again, I do tend to pay closer attention to regulars.'

Bluebird flew back up on the cuckoo clock and melted into the design as though she'd always been part of the clock.

'If you really want to sleep on the floor, suit yourself. But be sure to stay far away from the drawing on the floor. If you're too jittery to fall asleep, try taking two kinds of potions. That clear thing there will help you fall asleep – it's not a narcotic, don't worry – the purple potion is for good dreams. Well, it doesn't guarantee you a good dream, but it at least protects you from the succubus. They both just smell faintly of herbs, so you can take them without water.'

'Wh–why are you h–helping me?'

'What do you mean? You're the one who came to me.'

'You would d–d–do th–this for anyone who walks in h–here?'

'Like I said – regulars' privileges. Lots of people come into our shop, but you're the first to make it all the way into the oven.'

His words were cold and business-like, but the blanket over my shoulders was fluffy and soft, and the potion he put in my hand was warm. I sincerely wanted to be of use to the baker instead of just being taken in like a stray dog. But what use will a wizard like him have for a child like me?

'I . . . I . . .'

I didn't think that I should receive this hospitality

free of charge, and I wanted to ask him how I could repay him and Bluebird. I wanted to express my gratitude even though I had nothing on me. But my lips were too slow.

Thankfully, he suddenly asked, 'Do you know how to manage websites?'

And that's how I came to be the webmaster of www.wizardbakery.com.

'Okay, so I guess I'd be lying if I said I was a fan of hers. But I didn't know things would get this bad. I didn't mean for this to happen. It was supposed to be a joke.'

The girl sobbed at the round table by the display case. She was in a school uniform from the girls' high school next to the boys' high school I attended. Which reminded me of school. I'd completely forgotten about it for the past two weeks.

Three days of unexcused absences, but then summer holidays began. I called my mobile about three times on the bakery landline, which didn't show up on caller ID. I thought Muhee might pick up. But perhaps the call went straight to voicemail because the battery had worn out or Mrs Bae had turned the phone off.

Not that I would have used my mobile phone, but it would have been nice to have it on me. I wasn't able to take anything with me at the time. The only thing that I happened to have on me was the key to the house, which I always kept in my pocket just in case I had to run away. (And why would I need the key if I were running away? Why carry around the contingency plan in your pocket if your dream is to run away from home? Ah, the tragicomedy of the homeless.)

Assuming I was safe for now – and it had been a few days since the police were here – I left the oven room for a few hours every day during lunchtime to sit behind the counter with Bluebird. Still, I jumped every time the door chime jingled. Which was why when someone walked through the door today, I automatically dived under the counter. I came out only after peeking through the display case of candles, potpourri and other party supplies, and saw a school uniform skirt, which confirmed it was no one I knew.

About once every week, we had people like this march into the shop to complain in person about the products they bought online. As always, Baker looked either annoyed or angry. He seemed to somehow despise the people who bought his products. He never smiled at customers who came looking for tea cake, either, but when people came in with a complaint, he exuded displeasure bordering on contempt.

'So what do you want me to do about it now? You're the one who needed it and bought it. The outcome you saw is proof that the product worked really well. What customer service could you possibly want?' He put a large mug in the microwave and pressed the start button.

'That's not what I'm saying. I just don't know what to do now. I had no idea this thing would have such a horrible side effect. I hung out with her for practical reasons, but she wasn't a bad person. How can I go on living like this? I think I'll die if she doesn't come back.'

Baker wore a subtle smirk on his face, and retorted, 'Then go ahead and die.'

'Look here!' Uniform Girl got up almost the same time as I seized Baker, who's about half a head taller than me, by the collar and threw him against the wall. *How can you say that? What gives you the right to snigger at other people's misery?* I prepared the speech in my head and slowly opened my lips. But, as always, the sentence completed in my head struggled its way out one slow syllable at a time.

'H-how c-can you s-s-say . . .'

I could feel Uniform Girl's eyes on the side of my face. She seemed more irritated by me, the boy who suddenly grabbed the baker by the collar but couldn't get his words out, than at the baker. I fell silent at that look. It was none of my business how he treated his customers. I was just a temporary freeloader. Bluebird silently tugged at my sleeve to tell me to calm down.

'Okay, okay. You, calm down,' Baker said, gently pushing me off him. Then he said to Uniform Girl, 'And you – sit for a moment. I'll listen if you have something to say.'

With a ding, the microwave stopped turning. Baker placed the steaming mug before Uniform Girl.

'Drink this. It'll make you feel better. Be careful not to burn your tongue, though.'

Baker sat across the table from Uniform Girl and waited for her to take a sip of her warm milk. *This was what you meant to do all along, wasn't it? You were going to give this tormented, anxious person time to pull herself together, even if she happened to be a mad customer. So why do it with such attitude?*

It turned out, Uniform Girl bought a Devil's Cinnamon Cookie from the online store. She cast the spell on the morning of the first day of final exams, and gave it to her friend whom she admired but could never sincerely like. Her friend suffered from a horrible stomach ache during the next exam period, and wound up marking her answer sheet wrong.

Messing up her final exam, which would go in her permanent record, was horrible enough. But then came the worst part. The moment the friend turned in her answer sheet, she could no longer hold it in and relieved herself. The classroom was instantly inundated with the smell of bowel movement. No one knew what to do. Even the invigilator pinched his nose, grabbed the answer sheets, and hurried out of the classroom. She just sat immobilised in despair while kids whispered among themselves and inched away from her.

A few couldn't stand it any more and shouted, 'Why is she just sitting there instead of going to the infirmary or the bathroom or something? It's not going away on its own. You're not going to take the rest of today's exams like that, are you?'

The class representative finally got her up, handed her over to the nurse, and ran away. The nurse treated her with some anti-diarrhoeal, and she washed herself with cold water in the staff bathroom. She went back to take the rest of the exams wearing her uniform blouse and school gym pants with no underpants on, but it had already been twenty minutes since the next exam period began.

On top of screwing up two exams in a row, the entire school heard about what happened. She didn't show up at school the next day, and on the day the grades came out, she was found in her room next to an empty pill bottle.

Uniform Girl hung her head as we wiped her tears. Baker waited quietly, arms and legs crossed, for her to stop crying.

'I have nightmares every night . . . I'm sure no one was watching closely, but there's got to be at least one or two kids who saw me pass her the cookie. It won't be easy to see the connection between the two, but . . .'

After a few minutes of silence, Baker rapped on the table with his knuckles and said, 'Are we done here? I'm sorry, but I have to go. If you're suffering from nightmares, I'll make you a potion that will keep the mare creatures at bay. Sounds like a bargain to me.'

'No, that's not what I want. You're a wizard. Can't you do something?'

'Even the gods cannot bring back the dead. If you're so desperate, go see them.'

His tone and message here were similar to 'Go ahead and die', but Uniform Girl did not lash out at him this time.

'Please do something. This was supposed to be a harmless prank. I didn't mean for this to happen.'

'Don't you think the timing was a little too pre-meditated for your prank to actually be a joke? If you didn't mean for something like this to happen, why did you pay nine thousand won for two cookies, plus three thousand won for shipping? No one in their right mind would pay that much for cookies – not even at a seven-star hotel bakery. Why'd you buy them?'

'No, you don't understand. Hotel bakeries actually do sell all sorts of cookies that are way more expensive than that. Considering the uniqueness of your products, they are actually reasonably priced, oppa.'

'Don't call me "oppa",' Baker snapped, disgusted by her attempts at flattery. 'Okay, so let's say for the sake of argument that my cookies are relatively inexpensive. Are you saying that it is my fault for making the cookies relatively inexpensive and affordable?'

'No, that's not what I'm saying. I'm just asking if there's something among the many Wizard's Bakery products I could use.'

If there were something, how would it help? Which one of all the things that went wrong could it right? Uniform Girl was missing a fundamental point here, which was that her friend saw those cookies as a nice gift from a friend to the very end. She couldn't have found any evidence of foul play if she tried, but the girl did not express one word of suspicion or anger against Uniform Girl after what happened in the classroom and her exam, and as she took her own life. That was what Uniform Girl had to live with now.

'Didn't you see the ratings and reviews on this cookie? Didn't you see that it works one hundred per cent of the time?'

'Of course I did. I thought you'd paid someone to post fake reviews and make the product look good.'

'Okay, then. Let me ask you this: did you read the warning label?'

'That bit about how "all magic comes back" and stuff? I thought you were just saying that. How many kids would actually believe in that stuff when they buy these things?'

Remembering what Bluebird told me when I first got here – *'Once he explodes, there is no stopping him. Be good, and try to have as little presence as possible. Don't touch anything besides the computer and the products at the shop, and don't irritate him by prying'* – I feared that he'd lose it and upturn the steaming mug of milk over Uniform Girl.

At the hair-raising screech of chair leg on tile floor, Bluebird and I looked up. Baker was looking down coldy at Uniform Girl.

'Never mind. If you showed even the tiniest bit of remorse, I would have gladly offered my usual words of consolation, but I can't bring myself to now. And I have nothing to recommend to a child like you. Even if I did, I wouldn't sell it to you.'

Uniform Girl got up, pushing the table back. 'What the hell? What kind of business are you running here? All you care about is sales.'

'I don't need business from a child like you who won't take the tiniest bit of responsibility.'

'Fine! If someone rats on the teacher that I gave her the cookies, I'm going to point them straight to this shop. You're going down with me.'

'As you wish.'

Uniform Girl was about to storm off when Baker called, 'Wait.'

Uniform Girl looked at him as if to say, *I knew you'd fold*. But what Baker said was nothing like what she'd expected.

'May this guilt stay with you for ever,' he said. 'While it was involuntary manslaughter, you will never be free from the fact that you killed someone.

Anyone with even a smidgeon of conscience would be haunted by this, but here's another curse for you: you will suffer from nightmares as horrible as the deed you've done. Just when you think you've forgotten her, she'll pay you a visit in your dreams.'

Uniform Girl stood with her lips trembling, then stormed out.

Baker stood for a while and stared at the door chime jingling in a frenzy, and sighed.

'You didn't really have to say that last thing,' said Bluebird, standing as far away from him as possible. 'Everything you say comes true . . . I mean, I admit she deserves it, but what if she gets even angrier . . . if the police come . . .'

'Haven't you got used to police interrogations by now, after living with me for so long? Why the sudden worry?' Then he pointed his chin at me. 'You – time for you to go back inside.'

I nodded goodbye to Bluebird and followed him into the bakery.

I opened the oven door and looked back at him. With every wave of his hand, lumps of dough ready for the oven appeared. The oven on the left opened with a clank and fresh waffles were transferred to the counter where they were glazed with pumpkin-coloured syrup.

The look on his face as he made these sweet pastries was far from sweet. If Baker's mood had a taste or scent, it would have been close to spicy. He was nothing like the pastry chefs on TV who said that it made them smile to think of customers enjoying their creations. However, what he gave the customers wasn't a moment's burst of happiness, but power that came with heavy responsibility.

Baker said not to worry about it, but I couldn't help thinking he looked downcast.

Chapter 3

Peanut Cream
Moon Bread

I am sick of bread.

I happened to stick my hands in my pockets as I passed by the window display of the bakery, and felt four 500-won coins with my fingertips, just as I did that day when I was around six, standing on the platform in a sea of people pushing past me. Running my fingers over the coins, I looked up and saw the bakery sign.

Many years ago, I didn't know about Baker or pay attention to the shop sign in flowing cursive. I only remembered the smell of roasted hazelnuts coming from the bakery. All strong impulses must be triggered by smell, I thought to myself. The smell of money, the smell of desire, the smell of hatred, the smell of bread.

I pushed open the door and went inside. That's when I saw Bluebird and Baker for the first time.

Even after the thing about Rapunzel's dandruff and the cat tongues, I walked through this glass door every

other day. Since the beginning of the redevelopment
in the apartment complex, the convenience store had
to make way for an estate agent's office, which had me
depending on the bakery for my daily, well, bread. It
seemed like it'd been centuries since I last had a meal
at home.

I got sick of sliced bread or breakfast rolls pretty
quickly, but there were so many other kinds of breads
and pastries there. There was the apple cake with
chopped cherries and apples, which they sold by the
slice, and the brioche baked with generous amounts
of butter and eggs. The mocha cookies that weren't
too sweet, individual-size pound cakes, glazed with
almond icing and apricot jam, marron gelatin pudding
with castella and candied chestnuts, star-shaped kaiser
roll that's crispy on the outside, German cheese cream
cake garnished with fresh cream and pistachios, some
unknown pastry with caramel syrup and potato filling . . . his repertoire was endless. Budgeting on my
part was the only problem.

'You must like bread,' said the girl in the blue shirt
as I paid for my selection that day. I'd seen her so many
times, she was a familiar face to me now. This was her
offer of polite small talk to a regular customer.

I hesitated for a bit and then pushed the words out
of my mouth like masticated food.

'I-I-I don't,' I said, snatching the plastic bag from
her hand.

I quickly glanced at her out of the corner of my eye before I left the store. Her head leaning to one side, she seemed a little puzzled. *So why do you try all different kinds of bread every day?* she seemed to ask.

I am sick and tired of bread.

'The train for Yongsan, Yongsan is now arriving. Please stand behind the yellow line.'

I was six, and I'd never been on the subway or a bus by myself before. Mum or Father had always been with me. So I had no way of knowing that Cheongn-yangni Station, where I was left by myself, was actually only ten stops away from where we lived. I'd never felt the need to memorise my home address since I was always under the tender, loving protection – regardless of how superficial it was – of my parents, and no one had told me what to do in this situation. At preschool, I am certain someone told me to 'call 911 if there's a fire' or 'call 911 if a stranger is follow-ing you' or 'go to the information desk if you lose your mummy and daddy at an amusement park', but I'm sure no one said anything about what to do 'if your mummy abandons you'.

Mum had me wear a plastic bracelet tag one summer when Mum, Dad and I went to the shopping centre together. The tag was made of a wide, transparent piece of plastic that contained my name, address, and Mum and Dad's phone numbers in case I got lost. The bracelet bothered me, so I wanted to take it off, but the clasp was made specially so only Mum and Dad could unclasp it. My wrist began to sweat, and then I got a rash on my wrist. I started to scratch it, and Dad yelled at Mum to take it off at once and just watch the kid. Mum probably threw the tag away, and that's why I didn't have it on me this time. Even at six, I sort of knew that if I had had the bracelet, I could have grabbed anyone, showed him my wrist, and been brought home in no time.

Mum said she had to go to the bathroom. I said I'd go with her, but she said I should stay because if I came with her, she'd have to buy both our tickets twice to get back in through the turnstiles, and that would be a waste of money. She said she'd be back in ten minutes if I waited here.

I didn't know how to read the analogue clock, and didn't have a sense of how long ten minutes was. This abstract block of time divided into sixty microscopic moments, then multiplied by ten, was too much for my mind to grasp. I could read the numbers on the digital clock twinkling over the platform, but I didn't know that the blinking dots between the two numbers were supposed to indicate something.

It's been ten minutes, I think.

There must be a long line.

Another ten minutes have passed.

Is Mum doing a number two?

I'm sure ten minutes have passed for the third time.

I clicked on a red button that popped up in my head like a question mark, and played a few scenes from before today. What happened at home before Mum brought me here today without explaining where we were going and why? I couldn't remember the details.

A few scenes came back to me: Mum looking at something on Dad's computer, going through this and that, opening and closing various windows. When I pulled at her skirt, she quickly turned off the monitor. Mum anxiously pacing back and forth in the living room while talking to someone on the phone, letting out a cry close to a screech. The kettle and glass flying between Mum and Dad like a ball that lost its momentum in the game. A white prescription bag sitting on Mum's dresser. Mum asleep in bed past late afternoon. Grandma rushing in and wailing. People's busy footsteps as they took Mum away on a gurney.

If I were a little smarter, I would have understood the meaning of Mum's long absence and known that I could be sent home just by going up to a member of the station staff and giving him my name and my parents' names. But the station was too loud, too big, and too scary for such thoughts.

Cheongnyangni Station was on ground level, and it was open on all sides because of the ongoing railway extension construction. I felt like I could just jump down onto the tracks and run outside, away from all the people. But every time I made up my mind and got up off the bench, the loud dinging of bells announcing the arrival of another train startled me right back down. The trains did not scare me much, but I felt I ought to stick with the instruction drilled into me: Mum told me to stay here and not move.

So I just sat there on the orange plastic chair, swinging my feet. I had nothing to do, and I was bored. The train kept regurgitating and swallowing people in an endless loop. Repeat-play-repeat-play. Watching this over and over, my unclear sense of time became murkier.

A gust of wind hit me every time a train pulled in. I stuck my cold hands in my jacket.

There were things in my pocket that weren't there when we left home. Why didn't I notice it sooner when the pockets were bulging like this? A packet of tissues and a few coins in the left pocket. A moon bread in the right pocket. I couldn't tell how old the bread was, but the barely visible company name on the plastic wrapper suggested the bread had been sitting in the shop for a very long time, and that it was probably the last one left on the shelf.

I turned out my pockets and saw the truth. Seeing dozens of trains pass me by, I thought at first that Mum might have collapsed somewhere like she did that day when Mum didn't open her eyes although it was past noon and Grandma cried holding Mum's hand. But the things in my pockets advised me to let go of the idea that Mum was unavoidably held up – she left me here and disappeared on purpose.

So, where was I? I knew I was in Cheongnyangni because the announcement kept saying so. But I had no idea how far I was from home. Why didn't I carefully read the address on that plastic bracelet?

I didn't feel the need to because until that moment, home was a place that stayed put and did not disappear. It was a place I could get to on autopilot. The distance between the playground and our house, and the little directional sense it required for me to get home from the preschool bus drop-off point was programmed into my body. I remembered the location of the button I pressed in the elevator to get to our floor, so if someone asked me what my apartment number was, I wouldn't have been able to say. But home was a place my feet could take me on muscle memory, so I didn't need to know how many doors down the hall it was from the elevator, either.

But I didn't know that if I were removed even a block away from my familiar surroundings, I would be completely lost.

'Honey, did you lose your mum?'

A lady making Deli Manju at a stall next to the bench where I was sitting asked, too busy pouring batter and flipping the manju mould to look at me.

'You've been here at least two hours. Lots of people

pass by here, but if a child sits here by himself for so long, people notice. Besides, Auntie runs a business, so she never forgets anyone she's seen at least once.'

I didn't know how long 'two hours' was.

'If you go down the stairs over there, there's a station staff person,' the lady continued. 'Go ask him to find your mum for you, okay?'

'I didn't lose her!'

I climbed down the plastic chair and walked to the end of the platform. If I'd heard that before I discovered the contents of my pockets, I would have walked down to the station office without a word. But things were different now. The moon bread – emergency sustenance – and the packet of tissues said it all.

The moon bread reminded me of the picture book *Hansel and Gretel* I had at home. Hansel used his wits to return home with Gretel, but they were abandoned in the woods for the second time. The second time, the parents locked the doors from the outside so he couldn't gather pebbles to follow home the next day, so he left a trail of breadcrumbs instead, which the birds ate. Even though I had no reason to believe so, I thought I might be abandoned a second time if I were to return home. A second time. The very thought of it was unbearable.

I needed to know why Mum left me. Have we run out of food at our house, and must get rid of a mouth to feed? That was the first explanation my six-year-old mind went to. I lacked the evidence and level of logical reasoning to know for sure, but I got the vague idea that there was a connection between the reality I was faced with at the moment and Mum's prescription bag on the dresser. Mum might be sick with some terrible disease no one can cure. So she left me here without telling me so she won't give me the disease and . . .

Oh, grow up.

I sat on the bench at the end of the platform. It was less crowded there compared to the bench by the Deli Manju booth, but there was no structure around to shield me from the wind. I sat as the cold seeped into my bones and in my pores all over my body. I felt hunger.

Crinkle. The wrapper ripped with a delightful sound. The air inside the wrapper, insulated in my pocket, was not as cold as the air outside.

I poked over and over at the soft, fluffy piece of bread, too perfect to ruin by ripping a piece. At the same spot that had been picked at so many times, a small piece crumbled off. I put it in my mouth. The moderately sweet taste made me feel better. The breadcrumbs melted on the tip of my tongue, became as soft as gruel, and disappeared without a trace. All that remained was a memory of something sweet in my mouth. Before the memory of it could fade too, I quickly picked off the smallest possible piece and pushed it in between my lips.

I instinctively knew that this was going to be my first and last emergency sustenance, and that I had to make it last. My head knew this, but my hand and mouth did not care. One more bite, just one more.

After some time, I noticed something slippery on my fingers. I licked my fingers and tasted peanut cream. I had to eat a quarter of the way into the moon bread before the peanut cream appeared. I wasn't old enough to know about minimum investment for maximum profit, but I intuitively felt short-changed that the peanut cream appeared this late.

The important thing was that the peanut cream made me lose all restraint. I forgot about the saving and melting little bits of bread in my mouth, and took a big bite. A clean arc appeared on the bread. Saliva began to flow. My tongue and teeth mixed the bread and the peanut cream into a mushy glop.

I let out a satisfied sigh. I couldn't care less what happened now.

But the moon bread I wolfed down in the cold – it was probably the peanut cream that was basically a dollop of margarine that did it – turned my stomach. Late into the night, as the last train pulled in to spill the last of the people going home, I kneeled on the platform and retched up a thick pool of wet, undigested bread. A good Samaritan who just got off the train patted me on the back to help me out.

'Where's your mum? Your mum! Kid! Where do you live? Your address?'

Many people's voices rushed into my ears at once. I shook my head hard until the digestive system moving in reverse spun the world upside-down and knocked me out. I didn't know if I had a home, or if I only believed that I did, but I had a feeling I shouldn't go back there again.

Incredibly, I finally got home a week after the Samaritans carried me to the station office, even though I knew Mum's and Dad's names and my name, and that I lived somewhere in Seoul, which narrowed down the area of investigation a good deal.

So here's what happened: I slept for an entire day at the station office. The station staff were worried about me, but I didn't seem sick apart from the throwing-up, which had stopped. If they called the ambulance, one of the staff had to be responsible for me and take care of a little John Doe, which I suppose was too much extra work for them. Reporting and handing over a stray kid to the police meant being summoned by the police for more interrogations, possibly writing up a statement, which could mean having to spend their precious paid time off on some random lost kid. So they threw a blanket over me and left me in the station office.

The next day, the Samaritans from the day before

saw me still in the office on their way to work and threw a fit. They had a screaming match with the station staff, saying that they'd post about this on the Korea Railway website. They got me out of the office and took me to an emergency room. I woke up on the fourth day of my abandonment, an IV needle hooked up to my arm.

The hospital quarrelled with the Samaritans saying they couldn't go on looking after a kid without a guardian. I was conscious, but I pretended not to understand any of the doctor's questions because I didn't know how to get through this situation. The hospital staff lamented that I had amnesia on top of aphasia.

On the fifth day, the Samaritans paid for the three days' hospital fee, various blood tests and X-rays, and took me to the police station. They filled out forms and handed me over to the cops.

'The hospital wouldn't release the child without payment . . . We don't know who the child's parents are . . . We're unmarried and we can't keep the child with us . . . We can't keep missing work like this . . .'

The cops promised to contact them once they found the parents so they could be reimbursed for the hospital fee. But they waved their hands saying there was no need for any of that – *just don't summon us again.*

'Kid, thank these nice people. You would have been dead by now if it weren't for them.'

They shook their heads.

'The child probably doesn't even know what's hap-pened to him. Don't worry about it.'

I didn't open my mouth, but I bowed to them. That was the best thanks and apology I could give them at the time.

Thinking that they'd find it suspicious if I started talking the moment they left, I kept quiet and wrote down the names of Mum and Dad on a piece of paper as the police officer told me to. When he asked me about other things, I shook my head to mean 'I don't know.'

Mum and Dad both had names that were much too common. This was a time when they were still in the process of digitising people's information, so they couldn't pull up a name and a face right away. The biggest problem was that they hadn't had any reports on missing six-year-old boys in the past week. The police called every single person with the same name, but they had so many other things to do than to go through the list all day. The police officer who was in charge of my case kept being paged here and there, and I sat for long stretches alone in a folding chair by his desk.

On my second day at the police station, the cops finally got hold of Dad. When the policeman admon-ished him for not filing a missing child report right away, Dad said that he didn't have the presence of mind to do so because the child's mother was in a critical condition.

When I returned home with Dad, Mum wasn't there. Dad took me to yet another hospital where Mum lay in the hospital bed with an IV needle in her arm like the one I had a few days ago, staring up at the white, brick-patterned ceiling. She looked over at us when Dad called her, but she didn't seem to remember who I was. It suddenly occurred to me that she abandoned me because she really was sick.

The sleeve of her other arm, the one without the IV needle, had ridden up, revealing a clear red line on her wrist. Dad noticed that I was staring at her wrist, and quietly pulled down her sleeve.

After that, Mum spent about two weeks out of the month at the hospital, and Dad told me not to bother her because she was sick. So I stopped talking to her altogether. I thought that was the best way to not bother her so she could get better soon.

I seldom made eye contact with her after that. The adults often spoke in strange codes, uttering words like 'Prozac' or 'Zoloft'.

Three months later, I came home from preschool and found Mum gone and a group of strange men taking pictures of our house. Grandma was lying unconscious in one corner of the living room, the house stank of urine, and Dad's belt was looped and hanging from the chandelier.

Why is that up there?

I had no idea, but the important thing was that although Mum disappeared, I was safely back home. Mum was gone, but my reality hadn't changed. There was little difference between living with Mum's shell and not living with her at all.

A few years later, I came across several varieties of moon bread – Full Moon, Great Moon – at the school shop, but they were all fake. I could not find the moon bread that tasted the same as the one I ate in the cold that day. How ironic that I puked it all up and yet it still remains in my memory as the most delicious piece of pastry I've ever had.

Searching for some unidentifiable trace, I continued to find and eat cheap, stale bread that contained strawberry cream or orange cream. Once I accepted that I'd never find the Peanut Cream Moon Bread with that exact taste, I understood that Mum was gone for ever.

'Oh, that's right. You don't like bread,' said Bluebird, reaching for the tray to put away the buns in front of me. I looked up.

'I was so confused when you told me you didn't like bread. You came in every other day to pick something up. But now I know. You felt uncomfortable around your family and you were just trying to avoid having dinner with them. And that you tried so many different kinds of bread so you wouldn't have to eat the same thing every day.'

I slowly shook my head. Baked goods did tend to summon my disturbing past and present at the same time, but I felt I could begin to like the pastries here. Although he did put spices in there that could potentially be hazardous, his creations contained the future.

Chapter 4

Chain Walnut Pretzel and Marzipan Voodoo Doll

Bluebird was human by day and bird by night. This meant Bluebird's work hours tended to vary. She stayed human a little longer during the summer, and a little shorter during the winter or on particularly overcast days.

Whenever she changed form was when Baker's night work began. He seldom slept. He made the orders that came in during the day and packaged them for delivery to pick up. He usually did all this in the room inside the oven. When he heard the door chime, he came out of the oven and the kitchen to greet the customer. Since I arrived, I helped out with a lot of the order printing and simple packaging.

The reason he needed such a luxurious bed, it turned out, was because one day a month, on the full moon, he slept like the dead for a full twenty-four hours. He closed the store and slept a month's worth of sleep in one day, while Bluebird went shopping or to the movies like any girl on her day off.

I do recall that the shutters were closed when there was a full moon out, and I had to go home without bread. A wizard who can't perform magic under the full moon and sleeps like the dead. It reminded me of half-humans under an evil spell. Werewolves and half-monsters and the likes. What did he dream, sleeping in the oven room all day?

On her day off this month, Bluebird stayed with me instead of going out.

It'd been three weeks since summer vacation began. I knew I couldn't stay here for much longer, but I couldn't get myself to leave, either.

'Can't make up your mind?' asked Baker about a week into my stay, and never brought up the subject again.

When he asked me that, I'd started the painstaking process of getting a sentence out. I was on 'soon' of 'I will leave as soon as possible' when he put his hand on my head and said, 'You can stay here as long as you want.'

I knew from the start that he meant no harm and that he was decent. He was sometimes bitterly sarcastic and highly strung, and hurt people with the insensitive things he said, but he could be caring and understanding before someone asked for care or understanding.

A warmth like freshly baked bread spread through my veins as I thought about Baker and Bluebird.

I could stay here for ever.

No, no. My dreams don't come true.

At first, my goal was to hide myself, but I grew curious about them. What desire was folded into the pastry he baked, what evil clung to the sticky jam he poured on top?

In between registering orders that came in through the online shop and organising the list, I turned to see Baker sleeping in a corner of his huge bed, his forehead almost touching the cold wall as he slept on his side. I could put an elephant next to him on the bed and still have space left.

'Looks uh–un–c–c–comfortable.'

I was murmuring to myself when Bluebird poked me on the shoulder. She put her finger to her lip and gestured me to come with her.

We opened the oven door and went into the shop. With the shutters down, it was dim inside.

'He's very sensitive. He stirs at the sound of water dripping from the tap. We have to let him sleep, otherwise he'll be cranky all month, or at least all week.'

'B–but s–s–sleeping . . .'

Sleeping in that position is only going to make him ache all over when he wakes up.

'He sleeps like that to avoid the attacks of the mare creature. You don't want to be bothered on the one day a month you get to sleep. He knows how to make a potion that creates a protective layer for people, but it doesn't work on him. You probably know this already, but he's not the friendliest person in the world, so he has quite a few creatures that dislike him and try to attack him. He can get a restful sleep in that position. We just need to be careful not to wake him. Apart from making him angry, if he falls in and out of sleep, he'll roll out of his defensive position and leave himself vulnerable to the attack of the mare creature. And when that happens, the attack goes on all night.'

'D-does that k-kill him?'

Bluebird chuckled quietly. 'It might kill regular humans. They might go into shock and die, but he's not that weak. But he does feel all the pain. He involuntarily screams, "Just kill me!" in his sleep. When his hands get chopped off in his dream, the pain lingers after he's woken up. I've never had one of these dreams, so I wouldn't know, but it's definitely not something a human could handle on a regular basis.'

So that means he has to spend his life suffering from sleep deprivation and ward off things trying to kill him? The life of a wizard didn't sound like fun. *So why does a wizard like him who could probably make a living without bothering with customers opt to provide magical services and be despised for it?*

'Well . . . I'm not a wizard, so I don't know if I'm qualified to say this. Don't tell him I said this, but he does it to create a balance in the physical world.'

According to Bluebird, the world consisted largely

of the physical and the metaphysical world where scientifically inexplicable forces changed the metaphysical world all around the globe. The media of change were usually practitioners of folk religion, wizards and shamans. These metaphysical changes were created by people's resentment, and the accumulation of these forces brought about changes in the physical world, which upset the balance in the world over time.

Therefore, the wizard on this side of the world had to reverse the undesirable effects on the physical and metaphysical world that another wizard on the other side was generating, or at least try to stop the change from occurring. Conduits of magic all around the world had to continue this balancing act of doing and undoing changes, or collectively stop practising magic, which was impossible. This phenomenon would go on as long as there were humans in the world, and as long as humans roamed the earth, there would always be wishes.

'Here's a common example: an average female human can't overturn a car, right? If the handbrake isn't on, she can only push a car forward or backward. But sometimes, when a mother sees her baby stuck under a truck, she winds up lifting the truck with her own two hands. If you asked her to do it again, would she be able to do it? Definitely not. Where did her strength come from? You could try to explain it by saying there was a sudden burst of adrenaline, but theoretically, there's a limit to how much adrenaline can be produced in a certain period of time, and how great a physical force it can create. People call it a miracle, but we consider it to be energy that comes from the metaphysical world. Think about what will happen to the physical world if people could do things like this whenever they wanted to.'

The advancement of probability theory cannot go so far as to negate the possibility of coincidences or miracles altogether. If an unusual force is exerted somewhere, another force of the polar opposite pulls back the energy that is too concentrated in one area in order to create the balance we call 'ordinariness'. The laws of creation and extinction are carried out.

If something that must disappear does not, the universe finds something else to eliminate in order to maintain balance. This fundamental, almost sacred order, thus remains undisturbed.

In sum, life as a wizard was itself a destiny and karmic responsibility, far from the happy, easy life depicted in storybooks. But was a wizard obligated to 'protect the universe', so to speak? Why should they care if the balance is thrown off somewhere? Why not just sit back and let the physical world go to pieces, the metaphysical world warp, and the entire world implode on itself?

'Unfortunately, it's impossible for wizards to become bad apples,' said Bluebird.

Wizards had senses highly attuned to all the invisible

elements of the universe. According to the law of polarity, opposites attract like magnets. A wizard could detect the slightest movement of an atom within that magnetic field, and recognises himself as merely an atom in the grand scheme of the universe. As birth and death have little to do with free will, a wizard always found himself living the life he is destined to live, no matter how hard he resisted.

If only this so-called 'free will' could determine someone's place in the world, I wouldn't have ended up here. Like I always say, my only crime was existing in the wrong place at the wrong time, so why would Mrs Bae . . .

'The relationship between fate and phenomenon is like chicken and egg. If you look at it from a slightly religious view, you could say that all people and objects are there for a reason. But Baker has a different idea. Things with no purpose or will, that happen to be in the same space begin to reach out to one another, and that's when meaning is created. The meaning spreads and in turn creates the order of the universe, or fate. But that's just his opinion. You have to make sense of things for yourself. He hears the universe, but he doesn't know about everything that goes on in it. If he knew, his body and soul might be crushed under the weight of it.'

Just then, our contemplation on the laws of the universe came to an abrupt end as someone kicked the shutters hard from outside.

'Aw, crap! What the hell! Why's the shop closed? It's not even Sunday!' someone shouted outside. Bluebird and I rose automatically.

'What's this . . . "We are closed on the fifteenth this month"? You have got to be kidding me! Hey! Anyone in there? Open the door, right now!'

The chimes jangled as the woman rattled the door, shouting. She didn't sound like Mrs Bae or someone who knew me.

Bluebird nodded at me. 'Go on inside. I don't know what's going on, but I should open the door and talk to her. It's better than letting her make a racket and wake up Baker.'

I retreated into the bakery and Bluebird opened the glass door and the shutter.

'Hello, ma'am. We're closed today. We're all out of bread, and those are from yesterday.'

Over the glass display case by the cash register, I saw a woman in her mid-twenties push past Bluebird into the shop.

'You think I came all the way here and banged on the door for a loaf of bread? Is this the only bakery around? I have to see the baker. Bring me the baker.'

'Unfortunately, the baker is not around today. As it says on the door, we are closed today. If you are an online store customer, the announcement went up on the website, too. It's kind of hard to miss the notice on the home page where it says which day we're closed this month.'

'If you're closed, why are *you* here?'

'I'm here for just a little while to clean up. I'm sorry you had to come all this way, but please come back another time. Or you can post your question on the website, and we'll get back to you as soon as we can.'

The woman plopped down in the chair where Uniform Girl sat some time ago, and settled in like an insurance scam artist lying in the street until they approved her claim.

'I'm a busy woman. Can't you call him?'

'The baker is not at home, and he doesn't have a mobile phone. I'm sorry.'

'You expect me to believe that? Who doesn't carry a mobile phone these days?'

'Some people just prefer not to be bound to machines,' Bluebird said with a polite smile. 'Please make yourself at home and I'll make you a cup of coffee.'

Bluebird put the coffee on. She chose to keep the customer appeased and quiet so that Baker could sleep, rather than waking him up trying to make her go away.

Bluebird saw, just once, how Baker behaved when he was really angry. He punched the wall with his fist before Bluebird could stop him, and instantly set the wall on fire. The fire spread to the shop next door, and fire engines came. Being snippy to the customers was nothing. When I asked what made him blow a gasket that day, I got a smile in lieu of an answer.

The woman took a sip of the coffee Bluebird offered and said, 'I guess you could help me since you work here. I'm in a rush. I'll take whatever voodoo doll you have in stock.'

This woman came all the way down here to buy a voodoo doll that would arrive at her house in three days if she ordered it online. Who did she need to lay a curse on in such a hurry?

The voodoo dolls made here were a little different from the stereotypical human-shaped dolls made of rags. They were human-shaped confections the size of an adult male's hand, made of marzipan, nuts and dragées.

Inside the marzipan casing were internal organs made of all different colours of jelly, and approximations of bones made of long, sticklike cookies. There was a small incision on the front of the well-crafted human form where the hair or nail clipping of the soon-to-be-cursed would go.

According to the reviews posted online, one customer thoroughly chewed and swallowed every last bit of the voodoo doll to ensure a perfect, foolproof curse, but I would say the ingredients were too sweet for consumption, and most people would feel too squeamish to eat it. This woman here, however, seemed like just the sort to chew every last bit of it.

Bluebird smiled worriedly as if to ask, *Why the voodoo doll of all the products?*

'We don't have any voodoo dolls in stock at the moment,' she said. 'We start making the orders as they come in. It's not just the voodoo doll. Everything we sell is made to order. The curse won't work properly if you use whatever's in stock.'

'So, I'm asking for one right now. What, you can't make one?'

'Well . . . I'm not an apprentice. I'm just an errand girl.'

'And a useless errand girl at that. Can't do this, can't do that . . .'

Bluebird was being harassed, and all I could do was hide in the kitchen breaking out in a cold sweat, thinking I would only make things worse with my stutter if I tried to help. This was not right. Just then, a warm, large hand landed on my shoulder and made me jump. I looked up and saw Baker looking out at the shop without a trace of sleepiness in his eyes.

'They contain dark magic that harms the body, so it must be made with extra care. It's not for someone like me to make,' I heard Bluebird continue to handle the ill-tempered customer.

'So, anyway, if I order that thing online, can I stick a pin in its eyes and make someone blind? Can I stab it in the heart and make the heart stop?'

'Before you do that, you'll have to get the person's

hair or nail clipping. Besides, if you're looking for voodoo dolls that kill people, you've come to the wrong place. As it says in the product description on the website, Baker always leaves out the heart. No matter how great the resentment, no one should kill another person.'

'Shut up. How is it a voodoo doll or black magic if you can't use it to off someone?'

'What is all this racket about! What do you want?' Baker finally emerged from behind the counter. Astonished by his appearance, Bluebird covered her mouth.

The woman smirked and turned to Bluebird. 'You two were playing with me, weren't you? Baker's not in? Who're you trying to fool?'

'Stop,' said Baker in a tone that silenced the woman. 'If you don't leave her alone, there is no telling what I might do. You're the one who's trespassing in someone's shop and disturbing the peace.'

'Is threatening customers your speciality?'

'If you think that we'll stop at simply threatening customers, go ahead and try me.'

'Fine. I'm sorry I disturbed you,' the woman muttered, sitting back down. 'But I'm in a hurry, so help me.'

Apparently not completely awake yet, Baker paused for a moment before he continued, 'You want a voodoo doll. That takes a full day to make because a lot of work goes into it. You might as well go home. I can't do anything today, but if you live in Seoul, I can get it to you the day after tomorrow via quick delivery. You pay for the delivery.'

'No,' said the woman, suddenly desperate. 'The day after tomorrow will be too late. The police have already released him. He might already be waiting for me outside my building as we speak.'

'I don't know who this guy is, but your only other option is to sit here and wait until the day after tomorrow,' Baker shot back, annoyed.

'I'll wait here. So you're gonna do it?'

He hadn't expected her to comply so easily. He sighed and picked up the account book next to the cash register and started flipping through it.

'Name and address? By the way, you do have the person's hair or nail clipping, right?'

'Of course. Right after I ripped it off, I thought, this is it. My name is . . .'

Baker got her name, flipped through the list of online store members, and asked, 'Your ID ends with 82 and the last four digits of your telephone number is 7648, yes?'

'Yes. Is there someone with the same name?'

'No . . . but there's a record of you buying something from the online store four months ago.'

'Yes, that's right. I got a Chain Walnut Pretzel.'

'I hope I'm wrong about this, but you're not trying to use the voodoo doll on someone you fed that Chain Walnut Pretzel to, are you?'

'I am. So what?'

She looked puzzled. Baker closed the account book with a big slap.

'I won't take your order. There is a limit to how much you can mess with somebody.'

'Why not? Isn't that what you people do, anyway? Mess with people's bodies and heads? Why can't I use both on the same person?'

Chain Walnut Pretzel

2 per serving.

10,000 won.

Ingredients: walnuts, flour, dried yeast, salt, sugar, water, cinnamon powder, baking soda, olive oil and a secret extract.

Product details: Feed it to your unrequited lover. The duration of the effect varies from person to person, but on average, whoever consumes it will not be able to take his or her eyes off you for forty-eight hours. It is your job to win this person over while they are smitten with you for this period of time. If you are successful, you will form a relationship as strong as chains with this person.

Directions: About 5 a.m. on the day of use, place this product eastward before the sun comes up and say, 'Please bind [your crush's name here]'s heart to me, [your name here], and may the bond never be severed.' If the spell works, your hearts will be bound together by an invisible chain.

Please note that a bond formed through this spell is not easily broken, and that you should put a lot of thought into whether the person is right for you. Attempts to break the chain by force may result in injury to yourself.

Negative or positive, a powerful emotion should always be handled with care. The source of energy that ignites irrational behaviour generally has its roots in desire. As all religions have shown us from ancient times, powerful love with low boiling points often lead to aggression and violence.

If a person's emotions were lumps of dough, I would stretch my fondness for someone, if I ever fell in love, as long and thin as possible. As long and thin as a strand of noodle rolled out by a very capable pair of hands. Anger is the only thick, short burst of emotion I need in my life.

I suppose this customer experienced a powerful, short-lived love. She fell in love at first sight, fed him the Chain Walnut Pretzel, and succeeded in winning his heart. Her feelings lasted three months. When it comes to shelf life, a can of tuna often outlasts human emotions.

Their story, it turned out, began with a pretty ordinary meet-cute. He was a charismatic, sociable class president at a university and she was an executive committee member who looked up to him. As she was leaving the committee, a year later, she wished him luck with his job search and gave him the pretzel as a gift. She was still banking on his outgoing personality and his future rather than fretting over his modest family circumstances at that point.

The man graduated and turned into an archetypal example of the age of unemployed young adults, and his anxiety exacerbated his inferiority complex regarding his middle-class girlfriend. He'd been counting on his activities as class president and the networking he did at university to help him land a job, but he was rejected by ten companies in two months.

The inferiority complex was the cause behind his subsequent obsession. The woman started to get scared as he pushed for the relationship to move forward, advancing five steps in the time she took one step forward. One time when she missed a call from him, he went so far as to snatch her mobile phone from her. She tried several times to get it back, but the man was drunk. He knocked her over and erased every single number if it had a male or even male-sounding name while she was struggling to get up. Among the deleted contacts were schoolfriends, teachers at her language school, professors, and girlfriends who happened to have male-sounding names. She was angry and, more importantly, frightened. She broke up with him via text message.

And thus began his stalking. Her finals had just ended and vacation begun, so she went abroad for about two weeks to stay with a relative. God knows how he found out when she was returning, but when she arrived at Incheon Airport, he was standing at the gate looking murderous. She was being dragged around by her hair when a security guard came to restrain him. She made a narrow escape, holed up in her house for a while, and carefully snuck out today.

'Don't you think this is reason enough? It's not like I abandoned him because I got sick of him! I feared for my life. If I dumped him because he has no money, no car, nothing on his CV, and no prospects, then I'm a bitch. But I'm not vain. I am a hard-working student preparing for the Level-9 Civil Servant Exam myself, and I don't own a Louis Vuitton bag like you see every five minutes on the street. If I were going to dump him for reasons like that, I wouldn't have bought him those pretzels. If I chose him back then because I'd momentarily gone blind, I want to blind him so he'll never be able to see me again.'

If what she was saying was true, she ought to have gone to the police, not the bakery. If she was afraid she wouldn't be able to get a restraining order on him, hiring private security was also an option. But Baker did not point that out to her.

'Well, I feel for you . . . but that doesn't change the fact that you acted irresponsibly. I warned several times in the product details that you should give it a lot of thought before you give it to someone.'

'One can't always choose the right answer. Haven't you ever made the wrong choice?'

I saw a subtle change of expression on Baker's face. Was he thinking about the fire Bluebird told me about?

'The wrong choice itself isn't the problem,' he said after a brief pause. 'I'm saying you should take responsibility for the outcome of your actions. If you leave it to the invisible forces to clean up after you, the consequences of it will become even harder to control than they are now. And there's also a problem with using two polar opposite forces on one person in under a year. The side effects will surely get you, too. I don't know if you'll buy such a primitive example, but if you blind him, you will also be blinded through accident or whatever, in at least one eye.' He explained the horrifying side effects matter-of-factly, as if he were rattling off today's specials.

The woman hesitated for a moment and then spoke with a shaky voice, 'I have to give up a part of myself to make the deal. One eye—'

'*At least* one eye,' Baker corrected. 'The possibilities are endless, and the types of things that could happen are likewise numerous and unpredictable. It could be one eye, two eyes, the entire face, or your unborn child. Things in our world generally follow the "eye for an eye" rule. The pain you inflict on someone will be proportional to the pain you will have to suffer, so the question of which body parts will be maimed is not the issue here. Whatever your reason, you are causing someone direct harm. You shouldn't use this for relatively frivolous reasons like fear or justice. Profound loathing is the only justification for using the voodoo doll, and you will pay for acting on this loathing. Are you prepared for this?'

Isn't he getting a bit extreme, dragging unborn children into his threats? But as I recalled, magical beings in stories seldom hid their ill intentions. An ordinary girl receives orders from the king to weave a golden thread overnight. The wizard that weaves her a golden thread demands her firstborn in exchange for her place on the throne. The silly girl seals the deal without thinking twice. Seeing that she is later reluctant to give up her baby, the wizard gives her three chances to guess his name. She sends out spies to find out the name, Rumpelstiltskin, and the girl ends up with the golden thread, the crown, and the child. Magical creatures were often duped by human beings in these tales.

The woman was speechless.

'Of course, you weren't prepared for this. This time, do think long and hard about it . . . and that's the end of my speech. Wanna come back later when you've made up your mind?'

'Yes. I'll think about it and come back later.'

Baker stopped on his way back into the kitchen and

said, 'If you want, you can sit in that chair for a moment and figure things out before you leave. Didn't you say it's dangerous being out at night?'

'It's not safe. I think it'll be difficult for me to get home now. It's a long way away and . . . I was thinking about going to the sauna, so I suppose I could spend the night there.'

Baker went back into the room in the oven and lay facing the wall again. The pillow, so soft it melted against your head, and the quilt, fluffy and silent as a cloud, was wasted on Baker, who had to sleep curled up in the corner on his side to avoid the attack of the nightmare creatures. Instead of a sleep as sweet as rice crispy treats, his monthly sleep was no more than a catnap.

It was a little sad knowing that he could not dream, though he likely thought that human dreams were nothing more than delusions. He was a man who had the ability to interpret symbols and patterns in other people's dreams, but could not make that dream his own, for what we consider to be fantasy is all reality to him.

He helped others fulfil their infinitely pathetic, foolish, yet dire wishes, but had no wishes of his own. Far from receiving all the thanks he deserved, he was reviled for the unpleasant, unexpected outcome.

It must be nice for people to have someone to blame. Did that make them feel better?

What if the woman came back and promised to give up a part of her body or soul in exchange for the voodoo doll? Would you make it for her?

'That woman, she's never coming back,' he murmured, facing the wall. I guess he wasn't sleeping.

'She can't come back. A human body is a universe in itself, but it's not big enough that people can start giving up parts of themselves. Not even for love, let alone hatred.

'Nature doesn't care about intentions or backstories. I cannot control where and how accidents happen, and would have to let them happen even if I could. I can't always make people avoid choices that will lead to certain catastrophe.'

I could hear the helplessness in his voice as it softened to pianissimo.

'I know it's bad for business to say this, but . . . don't you even think about trying out any of these products.'

I listened to his breathing even out with the rise and fall of his shoulders and went back to the shop.

It was pitch dark. I couldn't see anything, but the full, warm scent of the bakery tickled my nose. I was starting to see that a place so full of such exquisite scents was a place where people could both find hope and destroy lives.

I placed my hand on the smooth melamine counter. There were a few little fruit drops for the occasional customers waiting to pick up their orders. I placed my fingers on the plate. The wrappers crinkled.

I carefully ripped one of them open. A perfect sphere and the taste of lemon rolled into my mouth.

People these days needed magic pastries for abstract and emotional reasons rather than physical, material ones. Overwrought emotions are invisible to the naked eye and could rise endlessly like a hydrogen-filled balloon. The similarity between emotion and balloons was that they imploded once far out of sight.

Compared to that, reality was so dry and depressing, like a swing or a bouncy ball – no matter how high it went, it was still within sight, and always came down, unable to free itself from the pull of the earth.

I was in a safe haven called the Wizard's Bakery, shaking my head in denial of the fact that I was falling back towards reality. I knew that I couldn't stay here for ever, and that I had to come down some time. I knew nothing would change if I didn't take action. I knew that I had to go home in order for this fight to end, that I had to confront Father or Mrs Bae, and that I'd have to go through an interrogation whose extensiveness might vary depending on what Mrs Bae had been up to. And that I would have to say I'm sorry just to keep this façade and structure we called family. But would Mrs Bae want to stay married to Father if she continued to suspect that I was Muhee's attacker?

I knew that I couldn't avoid any of this.

Sometimes, there was nothing you could do but let things run their course.

Reality was bitter, but the lemon drop was sweet.

The next day, there was a news report on a big fire at Herbhill Spa. The fire left twenty patrons and staff injured, and one woman in a critical condition. The police arrested a twenty-seven-year-old Mr Kim as the arsonist. Mr Kim said that he was in a relationship with the woman who now suffers from second-degree burns all over her body, but the woman strongly denied it. The woman received emergency care and is awaiting surgery, and is exhibiting mild symptoms of confusion from the shock.

Chapter 5

The Attack of the Succubus

Chapter 5

The Attack of the Succubus

Between that night and early next morning, after the voodoo doll lady left and Baker returned to sleep, the following occurred.

Around the time when almost all of the lemon drop had melted away, I also returned to my spot and fell asleep. My spot was always on the floor. Baker said that I could have the bed, that he seldom used it anyway, but I'd insisted on the floor for weeks.

The truth was, there was no reason for me to be adamant about sleeping uncomfortably when I was being an imposition anyway. But the ornate bedframe legs, the geometric patterns carved into the headboard, and the candy floss covers weren't what I was used to, and I did not want to rest there. Once I wrapped myself in that microfibre blanket, I would never wish to leave. It would envelop my heart as well and make me forget who I was and where I came from.

And so I was half-asleep on the floor next to the lab table where various liquids were boiling away when I heard Bluebird flapping her wings. The sound was rough and sharp, like blades cutting through air.

I rubbed my eyes open and sat up.

In the dark room lit only by luminescent liquids in flasks, I saw the figure of a girl.

Bluebird? No, Bluebird was a bird right now. Besides, she looked a little different from Bluebird. She was wearing a kerchief woven with blinding silver thread that did not seem like anything from this world. The kerchief was wrapped around her black hair as endless as the River Styx. Face as pale as snow. She was wearing a dress made from the same silvery material as her kerchief.

The girl had a beautiful face, situated in the area between life and not life, reality and not reality. She was wearing an expression full of derision and mischief rather than evil. Our eyes met.

Who?

I didn't think a new member had been inducted into Ovenland in the middle of the night. Bluebird's agitated flapping around the girl also tipped me off. It seemed she was trying to peck her or swat her with her wings, but not a single feather could touch the girl's body, which was so dark as to be blinding. She had no material form, an ectoplasm in the shape of a person.

To make matters worse, she was sitting on the bed, on top of Baker. He was turned over and lying on his back, bound head to toe in chains from medieval prisons. Through the dark, I could make out the chains digging into his neck and arms, tearing at his skin and drawing pools of blood. The chain must have been in the hearth, for the room smelled of hot metal and burning flesh. Smoke rose up into the void.

Red and green arthropods hung from every link in the chain and crawled about with their bristle standing. Baker, unable to turn his head, spat in the air. The stench of blood rushed into my nose.

This had to be a dream. *I am seeing a girl, Bluebird, and Baker in chains in my dream, because unless it's a dream I can't have yelled, 'What are you doing? Stop it!' without skipping a hint of stutter no matter how dire the situation.*

I jumped up on the bed and tried to shake the bugs off him with the blanket, but the blanket passed right through them. I went for Baker's chains next, but I couldn't touch the bugs or the chains even though I could clearly see them. In the meantime, the chain wound tighter and tighter around his neck. He seemed to have lost consciousness.

The girl, sitting comfortably on top of Baker, sneered.

'Move! Get away from him! You're going to kill him!'

I tried to push the girl aside, but all my arms did was slice through the air.

'Save your breath,' the girl said finally. 'He's not going to die. He'll only feel pain worse than death.'

I glared at the girl. This is a dream. This has to be a dream. No way I could speak so well if it wasn't a dream.

'That doesn't even make sense! Cut him loose!'

'Like I said, it's no use. I didn't do this. He did this to himself.'

'Why would he do something like this to himself? Who are you?'

'Haven't you noticed by now? What you see before your eyes is the image of his dream ensnaring him. All I do is help animate the images a little.'

She was a succubus.

A creature that stinks of darkness. One that sublimates dreams into dark energy. I'd heard that the succubus was a grotesque creature that appeared in dreams as beauties. Did this mean the girl I was looking at was also a dream? I couldn't find the line between dream and reality. This felt like a dream within a dream.

But why was he being attacked by a succubus?

'He and I have a score to settle. Thanks to him, the number of human dreams I am to collect has been cut in half. Since a long time ago, I've been looking for an opportunity every full moon to repay him with a nightmare. It's only fair that he pays the price for stealing my customers, don't you think so? He happened to be sleeping in a particularly unguarded position today, so I decided to intrude. He must have been having a fitful sleep.'

That was it. His sleep was disturbed. He had to get up and deal with the voodoo doll woman. I bit my lip. Baker had deep crow's feet at the edge of his eyes. The chains coiled up to his chin stopped the faintest scream from escaping him. The number of arthropods increased with the size of his nightmare and started crawling over his face.

'Human, stay out of this,' said the succubus. 'This man is stronger than me, so it won't take him long to recover, the way humans suffer after my visit. Of course, he will be tortured in his dream. I think I'm entitled to that much.'

The succubus pointed at Bluebird, still fluttering around her.

'She's ruining all the fun by making so much noise. If I want to make the most of this time, I'll have to take care of that thing first.'

'Don't you dare touch her. And let this man go.'

'But tormenting people in their sleep brings me such joy. When they wake up, they won't even know they've been bleeding.'

'Let this man go. What you are doing may not leave wounds, but I am looking at it right now. I can't watch this. I am a guest in his home, and I've seen the difficult decisions he has to make every waking moment.

Can't you leave him alone when he's sleeping? He can only sleep one night a month. Can't you just let him have his rest?'

That moment, the hand I could not touch yanked me forward by the collar. Within seconds, I was looking into the succubus's eyes as they burned with gleeful malice.

'This is between him and me. There are hundreds of others waiting in line to get back at him. I was able to seize such a wonderful opportunity because I've been flying in and out every chance I got. I'm not going to let some human take this away from me. So unless you're going to take the nightmare for him, shut up and enjoy your front row seat.'

'I'll take it.'

It was a split-second resolve that threw me into that space between dream and not dream. I found myself grabbing on to the wrist of the woman who seemed forever elusive. The corner of her lips twitched a little as she also noticed the change. This must have been the first time a human had ever seized her, not the other way around.

'I'll do it. Give me the nightmare.'

Perhaps I didn't think twice about making that deal with the succubus because I didn't have first-hand experience with succubi, but I think I'd have made the same choice if I'd known, too. All I wanted was to pay him back for everything he'd done for me, even if it only amounted to a tiny fraction of what I'd received. The succubus could come back for him again, but he would not be attacked today. Not while I was around.

'What an offer . . . I've never seen a human willingly ask for this.'

The succubus's hair-raising smile returned as her fangs bit into the darkness. With the sensation of eagle claws ripping at my chest, I was pushed down to the ground by the shoulders. Pain shot through my body from the waist and the loud crash rang in the room. She climbed on top of me and pressed down on my throat with one hand. Her face so close to mine our foreheads almost touching, I felt her frosty breath on my face. Her long hair smelled of pondweed in the bottom of a lake.

'Enjoy. But I can't guarantee you'll ever wake up. It was your choice.'

With that, as if someone had splashed ether on my face, I closed my eyes and fell headlong into a dream. I couldn't tell where the dream began. Dream within a dream. Dream within a dream within a dream.

I was six again. The floor was much closer than I was used to. I raised my arm and saw a large, loose shirt-sleeve, like I was wearing one of my father's shirts. Where am I?

The chandelier up in the ceiling, with its heavy curls and glass beads, somehow seemed familiar. A black belt hung from the chandelier and swayed gently in the breeze coming from somewhere.

Below the black belt, the figure of a person walked on, dragging itself. From where I was standing, I could only see the person from behind. But I recognised that sight.

I reached out. I tried to run towards the person. But I was frozen where I stood like a pillar of salt. I yelled, but the shout echoed in my throat and dissipated into the dizzying darkness. The person reached the bottom of the black belt and stepped up on the red plastic baby chair. Air escaped from the chair – *pshhh*. The person slowly wrapped the belt around their neck. I screamed at the top of my lungs, but couldn't tear through the silence.

One kick with the toes and the chair toppled over. The body hanging from the belt swung back and forth like a pendulum. The sound of scraping metal and plaster rang in my ears with every turn. Reach out. Your hands. I finally cut loose from the invisible force holding me back and started running towards her. I ran and ran but the distance did not close.

Mum!

I don't know if the scream made it out of my body or not. Mum's arms and legs swung in different directions like a dancing marionette tangled in its own strings. *See, Mum? See how awful it is? Now cut yourself loose! Hurry!* But the belt was made of expensive whole skin leather, not easy to cut through. The ceiling and the floor ran parallel, stretching on to eternity without anything else in sight, not even a wall. If only I could find a knife to saw through that belt. I ran in search of a knife. I ran and ran, but couldn't get so much as an inch closer to Mum. Her arms and legs twitched violently. *Can't I pull down the chandelier itself?* With that thought, adrenaline fired through my body. With my next leap, I found myself standing under Mum.

Yes! Now, to shake the chandelier so that the belt will loosen. I picked up the baby chair and climbed on top of it. The chandelier was as high above the ground as the top of Jack's beanstalk in the clouds. I couldn't reach her, let alone shake her loose. I remembered I was in a six-year-old's body. I tried jumping on the chair a few times before I came crashing down, chair and all. Mum's twitching began to grow still.

Mum?

After my seventh fall, I saw Mum's heels swinging in the air before my eyes. Mum had stopped thrashing about and was now hanging peacefully. Black liquid dripped slowly between her two stiffened legs. The stench was so pungent I could not believe this was a dream.

I crawled forward on my stomach and looked up. I saw my long-forgotten Mum's face. But I couldn't tell if it was the same as she used to be. Her face was far too black and blue, her eyes were about to fall out of the sockets, and a long, lizard-like tongue rolled out from her parted lips. Dark red blood glistened coldly along her tongue and fell, drawing a long sticky line.

Suddenly, I got the feeling that her eyes were looking at me. *That can't be. Those eyes can't see any more.* But every time I turned my face or moved, I felt the eyes following me. My sadness replaced by terror, I retreated, dragging my bottom on the floor. But this time, I couldn't move away from her. I had barely enough time to grieve before the belt came over my neck. Mum with her black and blue face came down from the chandelier and strangled me. Her eye sockets and nose hollowed out into large holes where maggots the size of rice grains tossed about. They poured down along the belt and ate away at my neck.

I don't know if such things are possible in dreams, but I passed out with the belt looped around my half-eaten neck.

I opened my eyes. I realised that I hadn't woken up from the dream but sort of skipped time and space to the second dream when I saw the happy family before me. The family seemed so happy that I was finally out of the picture.

Father, Mrs Bae and Muhee were sitting around a table. They were having a lovely dinner like any other family.

I looked down at my body. I'd returned to the same

body I had now, but Father and Mrs Bae seemed to have aged a little and Muhee was almost as old as me. Muhee's long straight hair fell over the shoulders of her reddish-brown school uniform. I see. This was their happy future without me.

The second I saw this, it occurred to me that even if I ever woke up from this dream, my body would never find a place to return to.

Hey, it's Oppa!

Muhee looked my way and gestured at me. *You recognise me as your stepbrother? Even now when we're the same age?* When Muhee came up to me, her eyes were nearly on the same level as mine.

What are you doing standing there? Come. Have dinner.

I shrugged away from her and tried to free my hand from hers. *What are you talking about? That I can have dinner with you and your mother? Since when did I have that privilege? If I return home, clamp down and just suck it up for a while, we'll turn into a family that at least knows to behave cordially when other people are around? Give me one reason why I should trust your extended hand.* There was a whirl of question marks in my head, but I kept backing away without asking a single question.

Mum! What's wrong with Oppa? Are you feeling okay? Oppa, you have always been quiet and distant, but you were never unkind to me. I'm always so grateful to you . . .

Muhee added with her cold breath on my face . . . *so grateful that I forgave you for touching me.*

Her face grew sinister and dark. *What are you saying? I never laid a finger on you. Did you turn a lie you told yourself when you were young into fact over the years? Look me in the eye. I never touched you.* My voice reverberated like thunder inside me without coming out.

Goodness, you don't remember me, do you? What a shame. After putting your hand up my skirt.

No. I took a step back. Behind Muhee's shoulder, Mrs Bae sneered coldly at me. Father's face was partially obscured by Muhee's head, but he seemed expressionless.

You pulled down my underwear.

No!

You touched me. You squeezed me down there like dough, and . . .

Liar!

. . . you came inside me!

Shut up!

Before I knew it, I was on the floor again. Muhee transformed from a sweet child to a girl who looks like she did time in juvie as she strangled me and spat on me. No, no. This wasn't Muhee. This was Mrs Bae. I thrashed about trying to free my neck from her grasp. Déjà vu. *(Why won't you help me, Father? Don't you know it really wasn't me? Don't you care if I die like this?)* I managed to turn my head and look at Father sitting at the table. His expression was still hard to read. Not disdain or hate, but not embarrassment or pity or regret either. An expression that betrayed nothing.

I was pushed back a few steps when Mrs Bae suddenly let go. At that moment, something pierced through me from behind. I looked down and saw something long jutting out of my stomach. A spear as thin as thread went straight through me and burst into beams of light. The hole became larger and larger, and my insides poured out in red bloody foam, a brilliant jet-black darkness expanding among them and replacing them as they flowed out. Wind lashed in the darkness and ripped at my bones. I grabbed the spear with my hand, which burned down to a stump. I don't know if I had veins left in my body, but it felt as though fire was coursing through them.

I looked up to see the three of them standing side-by-side looking at me. I lost my balance and staggered a few steps back, but did not fall. Muhee was looking at me with an appropriate mixture of regret and pity, Mrs Bae's lips were slightly pursed as if she were undecided whether or not she wanted to feel bad for me, and Father's expression was still the champion of ambiguity.

The sight of his face made everything suddenly so clear. Father had already traded in being my father to become Mrs Bae's husband. People standing on the other side of the line, me tottering on this side. We made a truly beautiful, moving family portrait.

You cannot grow new skin without being wounded first.

I summoned up power I never imagined or could believe I had, and pulled out the glowing spear with my remaining hand. As far as that family was concerned, I was the one who did not belong. Even if I did return, I'd be returning with a departure date already set. I was no longer afraid of returning, or the fact that I had no place to return to. I smiled in spite of myself. When I let the spear fall to the ground, the other hand also fell in flames.

Pressing on my wound with what remained of the other arm, I spoke.

Are you satisfied now?

My voice came out for the first time in my dream. Mrs Bae's eyes seemed to say, *Who do you think you are? How dare you talk to me this way?*

Doesn't matter if this is real or a dream. I have the strength to take down someone like you. However, from this moment on I choose to pity you. You already know I didn't do it. Your time would be more wisely spent looking for the real perpetrator than wringing my neck.

If this is how things work in nightmares, it's not so bad. Seems it's been a hundred years since the last time I spoke like this without stuttering.

I know that I didn't budge from the beginning. I rejected you and wanted to share nothing with you. That's because there was nothing I wanted from you. I thought that was the most sensible course of action for me. Whatever you've done to me so far, I'll think of it as the price I have to pay for my decision. It's too late to turn things back now. You can have this space all to yourselves. You can dream of a happy future here. I won't hold it against you for not including me in the picture. I don't think the animosity will get me anywhere anyway. But promise one thing: leave me alone from now on.

This seemed to irritate Mrs Bae also, who became flustered and tried to punch me in the stomach. Her fist went through the dark void where my insides used to be and came out the other side. I fell on my bottom and Mrs Bae's kicks landed all over my face. Broken teeth slipped out through my lips and I tasted the salty, rusty blood in my mouth, too real for a dream. But I no longer tried to shield my face or fight back. *Little more, just a little more and it'll all be over.*

Little more, just a little more.

I opened my eyes. Unusual for someone waking up from an intense dream, the sensation on my cheeks and body was nothing short of ecstasy. No wonder. I was transferred from the cold floor to the bed and lying in the sweet embrace of silk sheets like amniotic fluid. This is why I never wanted to lie in this bed. It feels too good. I wanted to dream on for ever with my head buried deep in these fluffy pillows.

And then, suddenly snapping back to reality, I sat up. What happened to Baker?

It was already the middle of the day according to the clock, and the succubus and Baker were of course nowhere in sight. Instead, Bluebird was looking at me with tears in her eyes.

'It's been two days.'

Two days? Really?

'We thought you'd never wake up. You were spiking a fever and talking nonsense even after that thing left.'

Bluebird blinked once. A big, wet tear fell on my hand.

'Your chains weren't as bad as Baker's, but you sure had quite a bit around your neck, too. It was choking you pretty badly. I was so worried you'd get sucked away in your dream, that you'd never wake up. But I couldn't do anything because I was still a bird. Baker wasn't waking up until morning, and . . . oh, I'm so sorry. I couldn't protect you.'

'What a-are y-you t-talking ab-about?'

And there it is again. How did such eloquent sentences come out of my mouth last night? Was it really all a dream?

'When morning came, the creature left as promised. But the ropes around your neck did not loosen up. Even Baker couldn't help someone already trapped in a nightmare. He said you had to fight it off yourself in your dream or you wouldn't wake up. Why would you do something like that? Why?'

'I–I'm s–s–sorry you were w–worried.'

Bluebird shook her head, wiping her tears.

'When the ropes disappeared, you were burnt out and barely breathing. The floor was slippery with your sweat. When I told Baker what had happened he was first angry at me for not stopping you, and then real-ised that I was in bird form. Baker moved you here and changed you into dry clothes. That was the great-est gesture of gratitude you'll ever get from him, so don't worry about it if he snaps at you later when you go up to the store.'

Not heeding Bluebird's advice that I needed my rest, I got out of bed. As I followed Bluebird through the oven, I felt the ropes around my neck as if they were real, and the burn of the fire that licked every cell in my body was still just as vivid.

Baker happened to be working on a sweet potato cake order near the office. As soon as he saw me, he spun around towards the sink and gingerly washed the cocoa powder and flour off his hands.

'Um, h–hey. S–so.'

Without turning, he dried his hands thoroughly on the paper towel.

'Th–that is. I j–j–just . . .'

Headlights instantly flashed before my eyes as if someone had suddenly switched to high-beam. The sudden blow sent me tottering back a few steps to stop from falling down.

Bluebird, who was watching us from the side, took turns looking at us both and went out to the counter without a word. The pain in my left cheek pounded through my head.

'Stay out of my business. What the hell did you think you were doing?'

The tension of the moment broke and tears welled up in spite of myself. Had I ever felt this way in a situation like this involving a teacher or Mrs Bae? My heart was so full of hatred or the need to get away, or grudge or derision that there was no room for such feelings. No place for the ache of knowing that someone is truly worried about me.

'There are two reasons why you are not dead. First, you were dealing with a relatively weak magical creature without much power, and whatever power it had it couldn't use to its fullest potential anyway. Second, you are young and the range of unpleasant or gruesome things you've seen in your life is very narrow. If you knew more about life or experienced pain to the extreme, you would not have woken up. You would have had the same vile dream over and over again in your subconscious even after your body began to rot in the dirt. These things affect your physical form, too. You would not have made a pretty corpse. You would have been a horrific thing to look at if someone dug up your body later.'

So the events that unfolded in my dream were

relatively mild because the pain I've experienced in
life was nothing compared to others, and so its mani-
festations were tame. But pain is absolute for every
individual. Was that all I was to him, a nuisance?
When I grabbed the succubus's arm, was it more for
my own gratification than his protection? Was it
just so I didn't have to see him in pain, heedless of
how he'd feel when he woke up and saw me in that
state?

'Learn your place. You think you're too good for
your world, that you need to meddle in other realm
business? Don't kid yourself. Humans have enough
trouble as it is in their own world. How nice of you to
come to the rescue when you don't even know what
to do with your own mess?'

'I–I'm s–s–sorry.'

With the back of my hand, I rubbed my throbbing
face and the tears that had fallen down my cheeks.

'F–for o–over st–stepping . . .'

The sentence, unfinished, waned in the air and disappeared. A moment passed. I looked down and saw a
pair of slippers lying shoulder width apart. I thought
of the countless times I stood as I stood now, waiting
for Mrs Bae's slippers to disappear out of sight.

But this time, the slippers slowly came towards me
instead of turning and walking away.

He patted me on the shoulder.

'Next time, don't butt in like that. I'm not going to

fix you if you break. Not that there will be a next time.'

That probably meant he'd never put himself in such a vulnerable position ever again.

'I don't know what made you so raving mad you had to intercede, but I was perfectly fine when I woke up.'

I knew he would say that. Of course he wasn't fine. I shrugged to show I was sorry for making a fool of myself and smiled faintly. Anyway, I jumped in because I wanted to, and I was pleased. As an added, unexpected bonus, I got a taste of what was coming to me in the future, whether it was a fight or just plain life. Little by little, the time for me to return home was drawing near.

'It must have been hard.'

Oh, it was nothing. Just your run-of-the-mill nightmare, I wished I could tell him. I was disappointed in myself that I couldn't.

Baker bent down and met my falling gaze.

'Still, here's my expression of gratitude,' he said. I could not stop crying, not from sorrow or disillusionment, but because I was so happy and moved. Was there ever anyone who showed me I was appreciated for what I was instead of misunderstanding, and by saying something so simple? This gesture also got me to recognise that I'd survived an endless night of hardship. I guess I'd been too ungenerous when it came to patting myself on the back.

Before I knew it, I was soaking up the front of the baker's shirt with my tears, my head against his warm shoulder. The chocolate melting in the saucepan was close to burning and the shortening was solidifying on the counter, but he was silent and still as he waited for me to calm down.

Chapter 6

Time Rewinder

The egg whites mix in with tartar in the bowl until it reaches a milky, creamy consistency. The sugar makes the froth fluffy and the almond powder adds a nutty flavour. The meringue squeezes its head out of the pastry bag and makes a fine wavy pattern until it reaches a clear peak. Pop it in the oven, and the meringue is complete.

But not really. This was not your ordinary meringue. If this were all it took, it wouldn't be a wizardsbakery.com product. Baker added a secret step somewhere. I didn't know the principle behind what he did to the cookies, nor had I ever seen what he did. Neither did Bluebird.

Time Rewinder, the cookie that turns back time. This was the most curious product for sale on wizardsbakery.com.

I could tell by the name that it was meant for time travel, but this was only an assumption. Instead of an image of the product, there was an icon that said

'Image Coming Soon' and the product description only said 'Coming Soon'. No details, not even a price. Of course, one couldn't add the item to the wishlist or the shopping cart.

So when was 'soon'? I was curious but I didn't pry. At first I thought the product was still in the experimental stage.

There was, however, a steady stream of questions about when the product would be ready. We had a stock answer for this: 'We are in the process of developing this product. We will try our best to make it available to you as soon as possible. Thank you very much for choosing wizardbakery.com.'

This was the answer we left on public posts. For private ones, Baker replied to them himself. The private questions were usually written by people with special circumstances and contained reasons why they badly needed a Time Rewinder, and a plea for a speedy product launch. Baker drafted responses that catered to the severity of customer circumstances.

The truth was, Time Rewinder was ready and Baker had shown it to me once. The product in question was shaped like any other meringue cookie sold at ordinary bakeries. It was hard to believe this turned back time until Baker broke the cookie in half and showed me what was inside.

Fortune cookie.

Most fortune cookies were made of thin wafers

folded in half and the pointy ends folded back to form a crescent shape with a hollow space inside. There, one could slip in a piece of paper containing one's fortune.

But Baker's cookie was in the form of a meringue, difficult to insert a piece of paper unless one could glue two meringue pieces together to form one cookie. Anyway, a canary-yellow piece of paper came out of Baker's meringue cookie. The edible paper was supposed to melt on your tongue tasting of coffee-flavoured chocolate.

The paper slip was empty except for the two words: 'Date' and 'Time'.

In your heart, find a point in time you desperately wish to return to. And then put the meringue in your mouth and crush it. Find the piece of paper and pull it out. (Eat the rest of the cookie.) The date and time you wished for would appear on the paper in red ink.

The most important thing to remember – and Baker demonstrated this for me – is that the meringue does not work if it is broken apart any other way; for example, crushed with hands or other physical force. One had to put the whole meringue in the mouth and crush it with the tongue. And after checking the date and time on the slip of paper, you had to let it slowly melt on your tongue.

The instructions – crush the cookie in your mouth, but be careful not to rip the paper inside – were not easy to follow, but the mechanism seemed so simple I couldn't believe one could really turn back time with that? No climbing into the complex machinery you see in the movies that requires expert operating skills?

Perhaps that was why it wasn't available for general purchase. When I logged in as administrator, I could see the responses Baker posted privately. I discovered through these exchanges that the price of Time Rewinder was also revealed only to those who quite desperately needed it.

With most online products, 'negotiable' prices tend to translate to some astronomical ones, but the Time Rewinder was on a whole other level. The farther back in time you wanted to go, the steeper the cost. That was why customers had to 'Contact Seller' for this item. Customers had to explain why they needed to turn back time, and when they wanted to go back to. The starting price, travelling just five minutes back, was too staggering to post on the website, and after that the price jumped exponentially with each five-minute increment that reminded me of the Fibonacci sequence. One had to at least be a multimillionaire to think about going back several days or months.

No one wanted to pop Time Rewinders just to go back five minutes. By the time people got around to posting enquiries on the website, their window of opportunity to right a wrong would have passed by far longer than five minutes, or things would have been progressing in the wrong direction over a long period.

The Time Rewinder allowed the user to set five different time units, but no one would turn back a whole year unless they were extremely desperate or crazy. The product was always 'Coming Soon' because expensive things tend to draw unwelcome attention, and the Time Rewinder's price was only revealed to the truly dire. Most people were discouraged by the price and did not enquire any further. It was too expensive to buy on a whim.

'I know what you're thinking,' he said to me.

Right. Going back a few minutes would be meaningless, and to avoid the path to ruin I'd been on for some time, I'd have to go back six years. Six years. 1,440 minutes in one day, 525,600 minutes in a year . . . I could hit the jackpot and rob a bank and still not be able to afford six years. The price for the first five minutes was ridiculous enough for me. It gave the saying 'Time is money' a whole new meaning.

'Is there a time you want to return to?' he asked casually without looking at me.

Don't ask if you already know the answer, dammit. 'Why is it s-so . . .'

'What?'

'Why . . . are you ch-charging so m-m-much for it? Like a g-greedy b-b-businessman who overcharges t-t-tourists?'

He sniggered and said, as if to himself, 'I'm no greedy businessman. I'm just a guy who charges a fair price for his products.'

'I d-dunno. You're like th-that g-guy who s-sold r-r-river w-water.'

He turned to look at me, a little surprised. His reaction in turn took me by surprise. Did I say something wrong? Did I just call him a fraud? His expression slowly turned into a placid smile, a knowing one that seemed to convey sympathy for the naïve child.

'You shouldn't concern yourself with that. And you'll stay away from this thing if you know what's good for you.'

'Th-that is n-not . . .'

I was interrupted by a sweet ball of chocolate he pushed in my mouth.

As he slowly lifted his finger off my lips, the chocolate popped in my mouth like firecrackers. It reminded me of pop rocks I used to buy at the corner shop on the way home in primary school. Those were cheaply made sweets, a combination of chemical flavouring and carbon dioxide. But this, it felt like the chocolate itself was popping without losing the smooth aftertaste of chocolate.

What's more, the popping sounds in my mouth weren't just random static. I listened more closely to the faint, muffled noise. What came through the random noise sounded like words. It seemed to say . . .

'Try the other two on the table and let me know what you think,' he said as he went into the kitchen. 'That would be all.'

I nodded at his back, trying to make out the sound in my mouth.

'You shouldn't have said that,' said Bluebird coldly as she punched in numbers on the calculator. 'It was my idea to keep you here, but if you say hurtful things . . .'

I admit it was insensitive of me to call him a charlatan when he sold real magic. But didn't he say meaner things to his customers and me on a daily basis? And he really was charging an absurd sum.

'Don't make me regret letting you stay here.'

'I'm s-sorry.'

'He's the one you should apologise to.'

I nodded. I thought the natural way was to try the other chocolate pieces and bring it up when I was giving him my product review. So I ate the second piece.

'Rewinding time looks easy to you humans, doesn't it? Something you see all the time in movies?'

No. No film ever implied that the science involved in time travel was 'easy'. Einstein's Theory of Relativity, the speed of light . . . Time travel scenarios in movies, where all creatures are living in the present except for the solitary protagonist dropped in the past, involved more imagination than science. Modern science concluded that time travel is theoretically possible. Possible but extremely difficult.

Realistically, 'passage of time' made all human conviction, struggle and desire meaningless, turning all things past into taxidermy, fossils, or memory.

'As you've said, it may seem ridiculous to tamper with something you can't see or touch in exchange for an enormous sum. But have you thought of it this way? Playing with time is going against divine will. It's very dangerous. Doesn't matter if it's five minutes or fifty years, the gravity of the offence is the same. That's the risk he's taking to fix time that has been tangled up by someone else out there.'

According to that logic, the time I was living in right now could have been pulled forward or pushed back by someone. His job was to put it back to where it was, and he didn't just do this whenever it was convenient for him. Only when someone made a desperate request and the request happened to coincide with time gaps to be filled, did he allow it.

There were other rules, too. Time-turning was permissible only under the condition that there would be no attempts to meddle with fate. It was okay if interpersonal encounters were affected by time travel, but the work of fate as relates to life and death was not to be disrupted. The amount of time rewound was kept to a minimum with the understanding that the work of fate could not be undone. The following case would be a good example:

Our child passed away today. She'd been sick for a long time, and it could not be reversed. We don't have the means to turn back time to before she became sick. Whatever savings we had, we spent on hospital bills. But if I could have one wish, it is to have her back for just one day to say goodbye and take her to the amusement park like she so wanted. It remains such a regret that I wasn't ready for the end — that I sent her away to the hospital amid the frightening, hectic atmosphere and the smell of chloroform. If I could do these two things for her, I'd be willing to suffer through losing her all over again.

The reason time was rewound in as small increments as possible was to minimise the dangers and side effects of time split. All living things from human bodies to individual cells possessed their own biological clocks. When someone somewhere on earth tampered with the flow of time, it created an artificial shift in the movement and alignment of the stars and the cosmic space, the impact of which was divided and shared by all living creatures on the planet.

The earth being populated by over six billion people, not to mention animals, most people didn't feel the impact of the change except for the extremely sensitive few. But animals had more keenly developed sensory systems and exhibited abnormal activities as a result of this impact. The occasional déjà vu we experience was also one mild side effect.

The moment time was turned back, a foetus about to be born experienced a reversal of time in the small cosmos of the womb, and a person about to die felt the raw shock in the natural flow of the creation and destruction of cells. So if time were to be rewound by several months or even years rather than minutes or seconds, there was no telling how the disruption would manifest on living bodies.

Time reversal also involved great personal risk. Using the example of the grieving mother, her purpose was to make her child's last moments a little easier. But with the reversal of time, the mother's memories of all things that happened since then were also wiped clean. She wouldn't remember making this request to Baker or the pain of parting with her child. To her, the time wound would not have existed at all. The mother would return to 'yesterday' not knowing what was to come the day after or that her child would die in the clamour of the ICU tomorrow. There was no guarantee, in other words, that the mother would be able to spend quality time with her child or take her to the amusement park in the time she so dearly wanted back. In other words, there was about a fifty–fifty chance that she would do things differently if she could do it all over again. If she rewound time and yet failed to do anything differently, she would probably return to the Wizard's Bakery website and (if she is an extremely sensitive and irritable sort) experience a tearful déjà vu.

So, hypothetically speaking, even if I were to turn back time to six years ago at risk of bringing the world to an end, I would forget everything that had happened since (or rather, those years would not have existed at all), and there was no telling whether I'd manage to stop Father from ever marrying Mrs Bae. I could end up spending those painful years with her for a second time (not that I would be aware of this repeat).

A magical item that did not guarantee anything – weren't the risks too great for such a steep cost? Once the terms and conditions were spelled out in response to their enquiries, some clients reacted angrily ('What kind of nonsense is that? Then what do you make it so expensive for?'), others acquiescently ('I understand. I don't think I need something so unpredictable. I guess I'll just have to go on a Viking ship ride with her ashes instead'), and most gave up.

And there was one more thing. What happened to the client's fee after time was turned? Did it evaporate into thin air? Did the deposit in the Wizard's Bakery account disappear?

It did. The act of transaction was also rewound when time was turned. Worst-case scenario, the client could continue the cycle of paying for the Time Rewinder and getting a refund over and over until the client finally felt the suspicious temporal jump and stopped turning time. For the client, the net price was nil. Baker, on the other hand, had nothing to gain even if the client was successful in making the right decisions the second time around. If anything, Baker and the rest of the universe would be physically and mentally affected by the changes. The Time Rewinder was expensive so as to discourage people from turning time on a whim.

I went into the kitchen. Baker stood with his back to me. The back of him reminded me of Atlas holding up the earth. Shortening, pastry flour, eggs, cocoa, vanilla extract. His hands were shaping a cake that would be shared in celebration of someone's birth. The baking sheets full of pastry fresh out of the oven were glazed with shiny caramel syrup. Why wasn't the universe created in such simple steps, like puff pastry? Why couldn't time melt on your tongue like coffee-flavoured edible paper? Why couldn't the spirit of a person simply crumble like a wafer and blow away? And above all . . .

'S-s-s-sor . . .'

'Sorry' would not come out. He wasn't the only one in the world doing this work, but his shoulders carrying the burden of the universe one individual can't handle seemed a little tired. He tilted his head in the 6.05 position as though he somehow heard my thought, his neck stretched as he lightly beat on it with his fist.

'Er, hmm, I . . .'

'What?'

Would you like a massage? Instead of words, I chopped the air with my hands.

'Oh, well, if you don't mind.'

He sat on the folding chair in front of the stove.

I rapped on his neck and shoulders and slowly said, 'Er, um, the . . .'

'Yes.'

'Ch-ch-chocolate . . .'

'Oh, that's right. Did you finish them?'

The chocolate was astonishing. The sound in my mouth as I ate them wasn't just static like a skipping record. The popping sound in the first chocolate said, 'I'm happy.' But it sounded like 'h-h-hap-happy' as if it were mocking me.

'It's not finished yet. I'm developing new ones, too. It won't be done for a while, but I'm hoping to unveil it as my new ambitious product for next Valentine's. I was going to launch it early this year, but the sound was all screwy, so I gave up. The product will be called "Festival", or something like that. There will be three sounds – "I'm happy", "Thank you", and "I miss you".'

'Oh . . . okay.'

'To make the sound clear, the static has to be raised up to supersonic, but the audible Hertz range for human ears is pretty narrow, so there isn't much leeway. Still, not as narrow as the range for bats.'

'Er . . .'

The popping sound was apparently not intentional. It was twice as loud as the voice, though, I'm sorry to say.

'You do like sweet things, don't you? If not, I apologise. I tried not to make it too sweet.'

I don't like sweets, not enough to eat three pieces of chocolate in a row, but I shook my head. And in terms of the sound, it wasn't a total failure. It suited someone like me. Too much static and buffering. But someone who's truly interested in what I have to say would be able to make it out.

I spoke, one syllable at a time, to the rhythm of my fingers squeezing his shoulders.

'It t-t-tasted . . .'

'Uh-huh.'

'. . . g-g-good.'

'Glad to hear it.'

'And . . .'

'Hmm?'

'S-s-sorry.'

'About what?'

'Er, the m-m-misunders-s-standing.'

'How sensitive of you. Don't worry about it. You're an average human being who thinks like an average human being,' he said as he lightly squeezed my massaging fingers.

'Er, s-stop n-now?'

'Yes, I feel better, thanks to you. But let's stay like this for a little while. I want to rest a bit.'

'O-okay.'

I stood with my hands on his shoulders as he leaned his head against my chest.

I wondered why a person's feelings couldn't dissolve like salt in hot water? For some, a can of tuna lasted longer than feelings.

And then I realised that salt dissolved in hot water did not disappear. Without forcible separation, it remained in the solution for ever and ever.

Chapter 7

White Cocoa Powder

The posting came up on the main page of a portal site.

Today's headlines were listed in the centre of the main page, and below that were the site manager's blog picks, most popular pages from the humour sites, and entries with most comments from the anonymous bulletin board in bold letters.

I left home with nothing, so I honestly had nothing to do. Orders weren't exactly flooding in on the Wizard's Bakery online shopping site, and without Christmas or Valentine's, business was slow in the summer.

Boredom meant increased idle websurfing. I lived like a recluse minus computer and phone games. I would have spent that time catching up on reading, except all the books in this oven were in Hebrew, Latin, or English.

So I happened to click on the link that caught my eye: 'Exposing a Fake "Magic" Store'.

It was listed under 'Today's Talk Talk', a string of sites with overwhelming hits and responses. It was

written anonymously, but it was evident from the circumstances described in the entry that this was written
by Uniform Girl who bought the Devil's Cinnamon
Cookie.

I don't want to quote what she wrote, seeing that
her choice of words was especially nasty. She conveniently left out the part about the misguided choice she
made leading to a classmate's death and instead penned
a detailed account of Baker's outrageous response. The
gist of it was that she paid him a visit at the shop to
enquire about an unsatisfactory product only to be
spurned at the door and later ignored when she voiced
her grievances. Not only did he refuse to provide
decent customer service, he put a curse on her, the
nerve of that man. Since then she'd been suffering
from nightmares and seeing a psychologist without
hope of improvement. The most infuriating thing of
all is the psychologist treating her like a loony when
she attributed the nightmares to the curse, she
bemoaned. The link to the website in question, with
one or two letters concealed, was clearly the Wizard's
Bakery website.

Thanks to her, the website servers went down pretty
quickly. The customer bulletin board was swamped
with profanity and slander. I deleted them as fast as I
could and put up a notice that said offensive and defam-
ing remarks would be deleted. The bonfire went on
burning for over two days. Most of the postings were

expletives written just for fun, but some were by vengeful former clients who'd been on the prowl for just such an opportunity.

Bluebird called the site manager and asked them to take down the posting from Today's Talk Talk. The response couldn't have been more unobliging.

'Only the writer can delete the entry. There's nothing we can do.'

'Even if innocent people are affected by outright interference with business?' asked Bluebird in a calm voice.

'You see, if the post mentions a celebrity or public figure by name, it can be considered defamation. There's also porn or sex shop ads, things that are too indecent or violent – X-rated stuff that we can take down with a warning issued to the user. But this posting has no cusswords so it isn't considered profanity, and we're looking at it as a cautionary post that upholds customer rights. If we delete the posting, it could be a violation of our members' freedom of speech. If the online shop web address were posted, we could take it down, but she concealed parts of it. We can't do anything about people who guessed the correct web address and ambushed your website. So without the writer's consent, we can't remove the posting from Talk Talk altogether, but we can remove it from the main page to maybe reduce the exposure?'

Baker listened as Bluebird caught him up on the

turn of events, and broke the long silence by turning to me.

'You. Get ready to go home as soon as possible.'

Just like that? Well, how else did I think this would turn out? Nonetheless, I was dazed at first. Were they getting rid of me because I'd only get in the way under these circumstances?

'Why d–don't I j–just . . .'

I'll leave right now. Nothing's keeping me here.

Considering the time it would take to finish the sentence, I left it hanging and turned away. In truth I didn't want to let them see me flushed with complicated feelings over my position. I was only a stranger to them anyway. The world turned dark before my eyes as if I were standing on a stage and the lights went out. Who was it that told me I could stay for as long as I needed? Why'd he even offer if he was going to kick me to the kerb at the first sign of trouble?

'Hold it.' Baker grabbed me by the arm. 'Not now. Tomorrow. I have something for you.'

I gave him a slight nod and went into the oven. The latch opened with a heavy clunk.

This was it. The entire time I'd been at the bakery, I had never meant anything to anyone, and now I had to return to where I came from. Perhaps I was only telling myself that I was preparing to return while actually planning to go on hiding or flee. Like a swing that's resigned to gravity's pull but wishes to remain swinging in the air.

Following Baker's wishes, I disabled all purchases on the Wizard's Bakery website and put up a new notice on the pop-up window.

'Our website is currently undergoing construction to provide you with better service. We'll reopen again soon.'

I printed out the orders that came in before the notice was posted.

Bluebird closed up earlier than usual and came into the oven. The weather had been fine lately, so there was still a while left before sunset.

'It's farewell after tomorrow.'

I gave her a vague smile thinking that it was just an expression, 'farewell'. Unless I am confined to the house forever after I return, I'll be stopping by the bakery, won't I?

Then it suddenly dawned on me. They were packing up to leave. They were going away.

Why? Because of one stupid little posting? I understood it was bad for business, but that wasn't reason enough to leave.

'I'm not sure, but if the police show up, we might have to move. That's how it's always been. Every time someone pressed charges, we shut everything down, closed the website, and started afresh somewhere else. We have the business licence for the shop, so the bakery isn't a problem. But our online shop is full of "fishy" things that force us to close our business periodically. Now that everyone's online, people press charges more often than they used to. Our website is based on a foreign server, though, and it's the only reason we don't have to shut down every week. What happened today – it happens all the time.'

Baker was trying to get me out of here before the police turned up. He didn't want to risk getting me into trouble, too. I couldn't go on hiding in the oven for ever, and if they were forced to keep away from the shop for a long time, I'd be trapped.

This oven wasn't open to everyone. To an unwelcome stranger, there was nothing in the oven but its dark interior and baking sheets. Just another oven. So if I stayed in here and the other two disappeared without warning, I'd be stuck in here for eternity.

'In the human world, our sales records and the customer's testimony are just circumstantial evidence. They can't pin anything on us. They can confiscate the cookies and analyse the ingredients all they want. They won't find anything. But once the police visit, they keep dropping by thinking they'll find something. That can be a bother. So we relocated here five years ago.'

'F-f-five y-years ago? Why, h-how?'

Did some customer press similar charges?

Bluebird paused to take a deep breath, 'Once. Just once—'

The sun was about to set. Bluebird sounded sober, as though determined to relate this story before she turned into a bird again.

'—he brought someone back to life.'

I remained still and silent as I gazed into Bluebird's eyes. I feared it would be rude to show physical reaction to such a story. But inside, I was doing a mental nosedive. *I thought he didn't interfere with life and death! He did this?*

That caused them to close the shop at a city down south and move here.

Since a long time ago, so far back she can't remember, Baker had been resuscitating dying creatures he could get his hands on. Bluebird, it goes without saying, was one of them. When Bluebird came to after a broken wing injury, she remained with him as a newly hatched duckling follows its mother . . . or so goes the story. But what bird would opt to fold its wings and stay in one place? She had no choice. There was a glitch in the resuscitating charm that turned her human during the day. It wasn't easy to wander off to unfamiliar places when she had to spend half her days in the body of a girl.

Success with many creatures made Baker more ambitious. In the end, a secret desire hatched in his heart. He had saved countless plants and animals, but there was one creature he had never attempted – man.

He knew that it was not only very risky but also forbidden. Every magician was aware of it. The death of living things is a part of the cosmic flow. When things that should be dead and decomposed remain alive and mobile, the flow of the physical world is disturbed. The change is so minuscule, smaller than a bacterium, but inflicts instant confusion in the food chain. A magician, therefore, knows to refrain from revising the cosmic principle of life and death.

Nonetheless, the idea continues to be a tempting one for magicians. The impulse to test the boundaries of one's power and to control the gravity keeping the balance between life and death was irresistible.

Once. Just once, was what he told himself, but what he really meant was he wanted to experiment once before really getting into the business of bringing people back. He wasn't conscious of this inner logic, but he believed he'd be able to save more people if the trial went well and gave him the confidence for future projects.

So what did he need to do?

He needed to find himself a body to practise on, the human equivalent of a lab rat, whom he could turn into another creature by mistake, grossly disfigure, or bring back only to let it collapse after a few steps. He needed to find someone who wasn't very important in life – more specifically an inconsequential person who contributed little to humanity.

'I guess his biggest mistake lay in the assumption that there is such a thing as an "inconsequential person". He let his confidence go to his head and blind him, even though it was just for a moment, to the most basic fact and the most fundamental principle for a magician – that there is no such thing as an inconsequential life.'

He found the body of a homeless man who had died not long ago and hadn't started decomposing yet, and sprinkled the white cocoa powder he made for the occasion into his nostrils, mouth and ears.

It was a success.

The problem was the first thing the homeless man did with his new lease of life. It is unclear whether his entire life flashed before his eyes as the hammered homeless man lay freezing to death, or if he'd vowed to take care of unfinished business in his next life, but he went on a murderous rampage that very night, taking five lives and then his own. According to the police, one was his business partner who sank their business, and the other four were his ex-wife, his two daughters, and the ex-wife's new husband.

The second-rate movie plot of a low-life, is what Baker told himself as he denied his involvement in the crime, but he couldn't pretend he didn't care when the police turned up and showed him the picture.

They were the fraternal twin sisters who were regulars at his bakery. He had a good memory for most of his customers to begin with, but these girls had made a real impression on him.

The girls put a lot of thought into most things, including deciding what kind of bread to buy. It was mostly because they were on a budget, but they were cautious to the point that it appeared their lives depended on their wise choice of pastry. He hated children, but he didn't dislike children who put such consideration into the choices they made. And he knew the truth about why it took the twins for ever to choose a pastry.

The older of the twins was attracted to him. She tried hard to conceal it, but it was obvious in the way she sometimes stole glances at him and in her manner of speech as she made enquiries about the ingredients. He picked up on it, grinned, and pretended not to notice. But that didn't mean he ignored it altogether. He thought that it was somewhat sweet, but that was about it. It wasn't as if he could get into anything with a human, but he treated her with the cordiality she deserved instead of coldly spurning someone who showed interest. He didn't give her his usual business smile. He was nice to her as an indirect and sincerely considerate refusal of a feeling he couldn't reciprocate.

When the police showed him the picture, he struggled to not let his expression betray him. His calm reaction backfired and raised suspicion.

'Look here. You're awfully calm for someone who just found out that your regular customers were killed in cold blood.'

The police found white cocoa powder on the jacket lapel of the homeless man who leapt to his death from the fifteenth-floor apartment after murdering the entire family. The powder was assumed to be a new narcotic and sent to the lab for analysis, but the trace amount of cocoa powder soon ran out and the lab found nothing illegal in the substance. Not knowing that this man was already dead once, the police traced the white cocoa powder back to the bakery.

Baker's entire stock of white cocoa powder was confiscated and he was summoned by the police a few times, but they found no evidence that linked him to the case. However, the neighbourhood saw him often closing the bakery to go down to the police station for questioning, and presumed he was somehow connected to the family murder case.

In a rage, he set his own shop on fire. That was the end of his human revitalisation project. He did not show signs of grief over the death of the twins, and had not once mentioned them since the bakery relocated to another city shortly thereafter. But from a distance, Bluebird was able to detect the toll shock and remorse had on his self-confidence.

Several scenes I witnessed since I came to live at the bakery made sense to me now.

'One can't always choose the right answer. Haven't you ever made the wrong choice?'

'The wrong choice itself isn't the problem. You should take responsibility for the outcome of your actions. If you leave it to the invisible forces to clean up after you, the consequences of it will become even harder to control.'

He probably wanted more than anything to bring the twins back. But to fight that impulse was to take responsibility for his actions. To promise himself that he wouldn't make the same mistake again, to shut that door behind him. That was why he was rude to his customers who made reckless decisions.

Bluebird had already transformed into a bird and sat on the cuckoo clock.

I had to go home when morning came. Not much had changed since the day I rushed into this shop, and in my heart, I was not ready. There was nothing in the world I wanted to avoid more than a fight I knew I would lose. The place I was returning to was not a place that gravitated towards some form of reconciliation and a respectable direction for the future. What awaited was rejection or violence that came from misunderstandings. If I somehow lived through it all and finally proved myself innocent, I would ask Father, albeit a little ahead of schedule, if I could leave the three of them and go live on my own. It was unlikely Father would allow it, and I imagined Mrs Bae would see this request as another open challenge to her

authority: *Will you listen to him? Do you see how little
regard he has for Muhee and me? This is all your fault for
turning him against me by calling him 'your son' and
invoking the name of 'his mother'. Now what will people
think? They'll say that I was the wicked one who pushed him
away and tore this family apart.*

I rolled out the futon on the floor and mapped out
my future plans in detail. How much money had I
saved so far? Did I have to swallow my pride and ask
Father for a small loan? I could come up with the
money for a room at a boarding house somewhere. If
I was going to find work, I would have to lie about my
age and get a motorcycle licence . . .

Huh?

Something rustled next to my head. A sheet of
paper. It must have slipped out of the stack of last
orders I printed out. I sat up and turned the sheet
over. A voodoo doll of a boy between fifteen and
twenty. Damn. I think he said these take a long time
to make. Would he be able to manage if I got it to him
now? It's not a full moon tonight, so I guess it won't be
a problem.

And then I saw the familiar address and name.

I stood for a while looking at the order sheet and
started to chuckle with my shoulders shaking. The
chuckle intensified despite myself. I collapsed as I
laughed like a madman. My vision suddenly blurred
and splashed around. Bluebird flew over and sat on my

shoulder. As I rocked back and forth, laughing, I hoped that Bluebird would be kind enough to slap me across the face with her sleek, soft wings. *Get a grip.*

You believe in this stuff? Or do you not believe in it but hate me so much that you need to torture some effigy of me? What have I ever done to you?

On the sheet was my address and Mrs Bae's name.

Chapter 8

The Precise Moment

I hadn't completely wiped that demented grin off my face. I mumbled something imperceptible even to me and pushed the last neglected order sheet towards him.

He looked at it and did not say a word. I'd never mentioned my address or Mrs Bae's to him, but he knew what was going on by my reaction, and in spite of it, got to work without a word.

Knowing him, I didn't expect words of solace or salvation from him. He was a merchant (even if his ingredients were bizarre), and he produced goods according to the sophisticated principles of capitalism. What did I want to hear? That he wouldn't accept an order like this?

But did he have to make it look so uncannily like me? Baker made a 'boy between fifteen and twenty' voodoo doll from marzipan as ordered. With the model in front of him, he sculpted a creepily precise replica of me in no time without skipping a beat. Normally when he was making voodoo dolls, he wouldn't

even let Bluebird hang out, but he didn't shoo me
away as I stood up all night watching his craft. I see. I
am the model after all, aren't I? Dawn came when he
was done.

Bluebird came up to the shop and froze when she
saw the voodoo doll. I gave her a resigned smile and
sat at the kitchen table next to my replica.

'This is . . .' Bluebird spoke slowly and scrupulously.
Stop. I know. He crossed the line?

Baker still had nothing to say. It was time for me to
buckle down and speak up about my decision instead
of waiting for someone to speak for me.

'I . . .'

Bluebird and Baker turned to me nearly at the same
time.

'I . . . th–that is . . . y–you know already, b–b–but . . .
I will d–d–deliver this m–myself.'

Baker took a good look at me, finally nodded, and
carefully wrapped it up.

'Okay.'

That was it. *Please, get a grip. What did you expect him
to say? That this is unacceptable? Unconscionable? Did you
want him to drop the doll on the floor and stomp on it?*

Baker put the wrapped–up doll in a large paper bag
and put it on the counter. The doll wasn't small to
begin with, but it seemed even bigger wrapped in several layers. If Father saw me walking in with this large
package, and found out that Mrs Bae bought a voodoo

doll, what would he think? Did Mrs Bae actually intend to use this? Did she truly mean to stick pins in its head or stomach each night? I was determined to confront them at least once in some way when I returned home, but a great part of that determination dissipated with the voodoo doll. She, an educator of so-called decent social standing, too old to buy into what people with good sense considered superstitious nonsense, bought a doll to slowly and systematically torture me. Nothing I say or resolve to do could have any effect.

'Excuse us.'

The wind chime on the door clanked and two men walked into the store. I instinctively sensed they were cops. That was quick. I tried to stealthily take the package off the counter.

'Put it down.' One of the men had spotted me.

I froze, still gripping the paper bag. The other man flashed Baker his badge and rattled off, 'We received reports from several places at once. You need to come down to the station. Are you the owner of this establishment?'

Baker cocked his head to the side and barely nodded at him in lieu of an answer.

'Sergeant Kim, take this all into evidence,' the cop pointed at the pastry racks.

'And you, young lady. You work here? You're coming with us, too. And you . . . are you a customer?

Didn't you hear him? Put it down. We're taking it with us.'

I held the paper bag closer in spite of myself. I drew it as close to my chest as possible without crushing the doll. The rustling of the paper bag clawed at my ears. I didn't care about delivering some damn doll to Mrs Bae, but the damn doll happened to be a voodoo doll that looked exactly like me. Didn't matter what the cops wanted with Baker – this doll would not work to his advantage.

'If you're not going to put it down, you're coming with us, too. Sergeant Kim, take that thing away from the boy.'

At that moment, Baker spoke slowly, 'You two. Cover your ears.'

I put the paper bag handle over my shoulder and covered my ears tight with the palms of my hands as Bluebird did. Baker quietly said something. I had my hands glued to my ears so I couldn't hear what he was saying, but his lips seemed to be mouthing something like, *Shut up. Don't move.*

The air changed. The cops stood still as though frozen. They weren't even moving their eyeballs, but their eyes were filled with astonishment.

'You can go now. Run. There's no time.'

His command struck me like lightning. I spun around and reflexively darted towards the door.

'Wait.'

He caught me just as I opened the door. I turned around to see something light wrapped in wax paper flying towards my face. I caught it.

'Take it with you.'

He didn't say what it was, but he did say he had something for me. I ran and ran with it still in my hand. Our farewell was the last stolen look I had of the two of them before I turned to go. *I'll take care of everything quickly and be back in no time, so please don't go anywhere.* But the 'quickly' part was wishful thinking.

I was deep within the apartment complex when I caught my breath and turned around. No one was following me. How long was the spell effective? They would probably give him an even harder time after being completely paralysed by a spell. If he hadn't used the spell on them, all of it could have blown over with a short interrogation. I put him in a tight spot all the way to the very last moment.

I slowed down. The tension in my shoulders relaxed and the paper bag slipped down my arm. Sweat evaporated from my palms as my hands relaxed, too. Plop. I looked down. The small thing wrapped in wax paper had fallen on the ground. I still didn't know what it was.

What was so important that he had to stop me as I was about to flee? To check that the contents were intact, I peeled off the sticker and looked inside.

I almost dropped it again. I quickly closed my palm.

For me? This murderously expensive object? A potential threat to humanity if used wrongly?

It was the Time Rewinder.

I stopped in my tracks and contemplated this cookie in my hand. This could just be a regular meringue. I can't see what's inside until I eat it. But why would he go through the trouble of making and painstakingly wrapping a single meringue?

Why don't I just pop it in my mouth instead of racking my brain trying to solve this puzzle? I brought it towards my mouth and then put it back in the wrapper. This was one variable I hadn't considered as I carefully mapped out all the scenarios that could unfold when I went home. I hadn't thought about when I would like to return to if I could. Eating this meringue cookie without a clear decision would be as effective as if I crushed it with my hand. It would turn the Time Rewinder into an ordinary cookie.

The time before Mrs Bae? Or before Mum hanged herself from the chandelier? Before I was wandering around Cheongnyangni Station? Wait, can I wind back so much time? When I've paid no price for all the time I'm winding? What about the crack in time and the impact?

I slowly began to put one foot ahead of the other. He gave me this Time Rewinder for nothing in return. This contained the most powerful magic he could perform. He had allowed it: *all the creatures in this world will share the burden with you, so wind up as much time as you want.*

As I walked on, a few forgotten facts came back to me. It was clear which point in time I had to return to. He said that interpersonal encounters could be altered, but not fate. I couldn't bring Mum back to life. Then my second choice was naturally the time before Mrs Bae. If that was too much of a burden for the universe and its creatures to bear, at least back to before things got awkward between me and Mrs Bae? What if that's too much, too? Before that thing happened to Muhee? But do I know exactly when this started happening to Muhee? And even if I was lucky enough to get it right, how could I guarantee that Muhee wouldn't have to go through the same thing again? I had no control over her life.

Whenever it was, I figured it wasn't something I could figure out standing in the street, and started towards our building in the distance. I told myself it wouldn't be too late if I had my showdown with Mrs Bae today, gauged her reaction, and then decided when to return to. The power in my hand was cosmic. I wouldn't use it for something as little as avoiding an unpleasant encounter.

Should I ring the doorbell? Considering the time, probably no one's home.

Father was often at the office on Saturdays, and Mrs Bae's school vacation was likely over by now. The apartment key that had been in my pocket all along felt warm. I turned the key as quietly as possible in case there was someone at home. I wasn't there to steal anything, so it didn't matter if anyone heard me come in. But as I recall, I'd always come and gone quietly like a burglar. I'd once read a book or watched a movie about the resident and the burglar living in the same house without being aware of each other's presence. How we'd endeavoured not to make eye contact with each other in this small apartment.

No one was at fault. From the start, we'd already made up our minds about how to deal with each other instead of trying to make nice and get along. Mrs Bae chose control and harassment, and I chose cynicism and indifference. Mrs Bae's actions were a little mis-guided, but those were her own endeavours to become my mother (her idea of motherhood was having com-plete control, but nevertheless). If I had harboured no hint of resentment towards Father's decision and simply gone along with everything she desired in compliance with traditional family form and values, would things have turned out differently?

Perhaps not, I thought as I took in the scene unfold-ing before my eyes.

I had closed the front door noiselessly and was moving past my room, the kitchen area, and the dining table. Up to that point, I thought there was no one home. I should have stopped looking around the house then. I shouldn't have stepped into the living room which was, as Mrs Bae so plainly put it, 'her territory'. I should have slipped into my room right by the front door and closed the door. But I instinctively turned towards the faint but miserable and unpleasant sound coming from inside the house and traced it to the master bedroom.

Muhee was sitting on the bed with her head leaning against the window behind. She was frowning and muttering something to herself. A man whose back was turned to me had his hand down Muhee's pants. I had to help her. I had to scream and get him away from her, whoever he was.

But as if my stuttering had been practice for this moment, my throat seized up altogether. I couldn't manage to squeeze out a single sound. At that moment, Muhee saw me. She let out a sharp monosyllabic cry and hit the man on the shoulder. Understanding what it meant, the man lifted his head and turned towards me.

His expression full of what seemed like confusion or horror, Father saw me. I was probably making the same face. Father's face expressed every conceivable emotion and desire known to mankind, Muhee straightened out but stayed in the room, afraid to run out past me, and the paper bag slipped off my shoulder.

It all made sense now. Why Father's face remained so expressionless even in my dreams as I faced the accusations. 'She'll forever be associated with bad rumours. Don't blow it out of proportion . . .' was his unfeelingly practical advice. I finally knew where he was coming from.

'Ah, ah, ah . . .'

It's coming out. Please come out, please. But it was as if a hand was reaching up from inside and pulling my vocal cords down into the abyss and drowning all sound with them.

'What's going on?' a hair-raising voice slithered up my back and above my shoulders. Mrs Bae had appeared behind me as I stood in the doorway looking on in a state of shock. She stood motionless for a few seconds, letting the situation sink in.

She then pushed me aside and strode into the room. I rammed my arm against the threshold and dropped the Time Rewinder. It fell to the floor, looking no different from a regular meringue, scattering fine meringue powder around it.

Mrs Bae seized Father by the collar and started to shake him without saying a word. It must have been difficult to find words after what she saw.

'Y-y-you . . .' (That wasn't me this time.)

Father slowly turned away to avoid her gaze. But to his left were Muhee's blank eyes stripped of all feeling, and to his right was me, too befuddled to find the appropriate reaction. *Father, just look at the face in front of you. It's all over and it's the least you can do.*

'You fuuuuuuuck!!'

Mrs Bae pushed him over on his back and started to throw at him everything in the bedroom she could get her hands on. She started with pillows and books and then moved on to heavier objects such as the remote control, desk clock, cosmetic bottles, night stand, etc. The lotion bottle got Father right in the forehead and made him bleed, and debris from the desk clock that hit the wall nipped Muhee in the leg. Another bottle from the dresser shattered against the wardrobe door and the room was instantly inundated with the smell of lavender, comically sweet given the situation.

'Now calm down, and . . .' Father's low voice was cut off by Mrs Bae's screaming.

'Calm down? You have some fucking nerve!' she cried as she ripped her own hair out.

With one sweep of her arm over the dressing table, everything on it fell to the floor and broke to pieces. An eyebrow knife happened to be in the make-up pencil holder. It wasn't a lethal weapon, but Mrs Bae grabbed it and turned to Father. *What are you going to do with it?* If I were a proper son, I would have thrown myself between the two of them and stopped her from slitting his jugular vein, on the off-chance that she found it, but I had no filial loyalty left in me.

Then Mrs Bae suddenly noticed me standing there like wallpaper and came towards me. *Wait. Why me again? You just saw it wasn't me . . .* Or, Mrs Bae had just found the last piece of the puzzle in her absolutely topsy-turvy head, that completed the scenario that the father and son were accomplices in this incestuous rape case.

Now. I have to turn time right now. I had not foreseen this. I was expecting normal, logical conversations with the usual sarcasm, so to be faced with a situation like this . . . *Please don't.*

'You bastard! It's all your fault!'

But why, why is it all my fault? Mrs Bae seemed to lunge towards me in slow motion. I bent down to pick up the Time Rewinder. *I have to put it in my mouth. I have to crush it. Wait, when am I going back to? Which year? When was it that we first met? Aw, fuck!* All of these thoughts flashed through my head in a matter of split seconds as I found myself yelling.

'Go back! Go back! Go back! Go back! Go back!'

If Yes

The face looked somehow familiar. An acquaintance from another life?

Father picked one photo out of four or five Grandma brought back from Club Rewed. I felt I'd seen that face before. Perhaps a long time ago, before I was born, maybe in the Mesozoic Era when the dinosaurs ruled the earth with their ponderous footsteps. Her face had no features that particularly stood out and it sure wasn't a memorable face, so why did I remember her?

Her eyes and lips a perfect line that ran parallel to each other, she seemed neither happy nor angry. Her face was neither pretty nor plain. Perhaps she looked familiar because I'd seen so many faces like hers around the neighbourhood.

Grandma let out a sigh of relief as though she had her heart set on that one.

'You've made the right decision. Forget about the boy's mother and start fresh. A youngish man struggling to raise a child on his own . . . people talk. This woman is not a widow. She's a divorcée but you don't have to worry about that. It wasn't her fault. Her husband got himself into stock and was nearly two hundred million in debt. She'll be good to a hardworking man who's not into gambling or women.'

Grandma looked through the files and pushed up her glasses, trying to remember the specifics of the woman's personal history.

'She has a young daughter. Takes after her mother. Pretty.' She gave me a passing glance as she said, 'She'll get along fine with the boy. She's a schoolteacher, so you won't find someone more fair-minded than this. You know how these things are. If the wife's a teacher, you're set for life. Teachers receive a pension until the day they die. You think your work will take care of you like that? She's a good cook and smart as a whip when it comes to running a home. She took cooking lessons in bride school when she first got married, I hear. She's so devoted to the elders in the family that she took care of her in-laws' memorial rites even after the divorce, so that's a relief. Of course, she'll stop honouring her former in-laws' rites when she remarries. You can stop sizing her up and set the date. We'll arrange to meet her family and take care of all the rest in due course. You're a widower and a mid-level employee at a company no one's heard of. If you reject a primary schoolteacher, people will think you're full of yourself.'

Father took the file folder and thumbed through full-body, profile and front close-up pictures of the woman, and then looked at the attached documents. College Diploma and transcript, certificate of employment at the primary school where she currently worked, a relatively clean financial statement, and a handwritten account of why her first marriage didn't work out, and the like. In the stack of paperwork, the woman revealed everything about herself like a gutted fish.

Father casually pushed the full-body shot towards me as I sat next to him eating ice cream.

'Take a look. She might be your mother someday,' said Father playfully, which annoyed Grandma.

'Stop that. He doesn't need to see this. What does he know?'

'Mother, I think that he has the right to see. I'm not saying I'll leave the decision up to him or even give him a vote. What's the harm in looking at a picture of his future mother?'

I took a sideways glance at the photo. I could tell that Father heeded Grandma's tastes by choosing the least attractive of the bunch. She did say to Father as she pulled out the files, 'A pretty face on a bitch is nothing but trouble for the family. You need someone easy-going and not revolting to look at.'

The inexplicable sensation I had when I first saw her image remained and grew with time. I turned my gaze from the picture. Grandma clicked her tongue a few times as though she found the situation pitiful and gathered the files.

'Enough said. Choose her. I'll let the agency know. Leave your weekend open. I'll tell them you're meeting at Jongno 3-ga.'

'I'll clear my schedule for the weekend, but don't tell them I've made up my mind yet. I'll have to meet her first.'

'What is the problem? I brought all these files over so you could make a decision without meeting them,' she grumbled as she retreated from the kitchen table.

'I'm off!' I announce to the empty house before I head out. My voice bounces around the apartment stripped of everything except the bare necessities. I always remember to announce myself as a sort of ritual in the apartment without anyone to answer back, to try to forget that no one lives here except me.

I'm on my way out with the clothes and the funds held in custody that Grandma wired me.

It was last year that Father was arrested for molesting a girl, and it will be another year before he returns to this house. It was Children's Day, of all days. New Year's, Thanksgiving, Christmas and other peak seasons for children's products aside, there were the regular character expos at Coex around the holidays. Father was always the person on the scene and where he did business was also the scene of his crimes.

Thanks to him, I have to transfer to a school far away next week.

Grandma said that Father turned out this way because of me.

Six years earlier, Father did not marry the woman in the picture. Grandma flew into a rage and stormed off saying, 'Don't even think about showing your face at Thanksgiving before you find yourself a woman.'

There was no reason. There probably was one, but I don't know what it was. But after the woman in the picture visited us with her daughter, I was moved by some unknown force to shake my head at Father, who told me to stay out of it because he was marrying her no matter what.

'No. I don't want you to.'

The words, 'I don't care. Do what you want,' almost came out of my mouth. But from some place deeper than my throat, a place deep in my heart, someone was sending warning signals. *Be careful. Think about it.* I thought this was no ordinary omen, and I could not banish the unsettling déjà vu with such an ordinary face. Strange, why do I have such a vivid memory of someone I may have passed by at the neighbourhood supermarket? I couldn't trust my intuition completely until I met the daughter and was convinced that I'd seen the pair somewhere before.

'Have we met?'

The lady who brought her daughter shrugged. She didn't know what I was talking about.

'Well, I don't know. Do I remind you of someone? It doesn't matter if you have seen me before, does it?'

Her head tilted to one side, she smiled.

True. It didn't matter if I'd seen her or not. But that only applies to when that feeling has no colour, form, taste, or smell.

I'd never once expressed my opinion since Mum passed away. So when I gave Father my answer, he let out a nervous laugh and then gave me a hearty pat on the back.

'You silly kid, this is grown-up stuff. You don't get a say. To tell the truth, well, I'm not getting married because I want to. I know you miss your mum a lot, but . . . Think of it this way: how many times did Mum abandon you? Did she deserve to be your mother? She doesn't deserve to be missed. You should direct your affections towards someone who's alive and standing before you.'

No, no. Please stop treating me like a child. I'm not doing this for some stupid reason like grief and longing. I have a bad feeling about this. I can't tell you exactly what it is, but when I look at this lady's picture, I get a knot in my stomach, my bones ache as if it is sending me some sort of warning signal, every cell in my body screams, neurons blaze, and everything just screams, *Stop them! Stop them!*

'You may not like her now, but you should try to get along. I'll bring her by again soon. She'll grow on you.'

'No, I don't want it. Don't.'

'What is the matter with you? Give me a reason!'

'I don't know. I just . . . just don't like her! Don't marry her!'

'So you want me to be alone for the rest of my life? This isn't just about me. What about you? Do you like having undercooked rice and unsubstantial dishes day after day? What about your damp, wrinkled clothes? There's only so much the maid can do. You like having no one to greet you when you come home?'

'That's a terrible reason to get married.'

'You got some mouth on you. Where did a little kid like you learn to talk like that? I've got to get rid of the TV.'

Judging from Father's unyielding idea of how a wife or a mother should be and other episodes I'd witnessed, I could somewhat understand without having it all explained to me why Mum abandoned me and even her own life.

In recalling the past, Father only emphasised that Mum left me at the station and omitted the fact that he did not report me as missing, and left out the circumstances leading to it, assuming I hadn't picked up on anything. I remembered Mum looking through Father's computer and quickly turning off the monitor when I walked in. When she suddenly held me tight in her arms I'd heard her heart racing. I also remembered Mum quarrelling with a strange woman who brought her child, and then Father dragging Mum around the living room by her hair. Why was he conveniently pretending none of it ever happened?

'Well, the kid is adamant about it. Mother! Stop it! I've never exactly been a great father, but I think there's a reason why a kid who normally never says boo about anything keeps arguing like this. I guess it's not time yet. Yes. What did I say? I know you and I have the final say in the matter. But I never said that I wouldn't take his opinion into consideration. So we'll put it off for another time. Don't pester the child. He's not ready.'

So that was the one time Father listened to me. And the result of that one time was this. All in all, not the best of situations – the Holy Trinity of shame, ignominy and inconvenience.

I wonder how things could have turned out differently if I hadn't stopped Father then. Perhaps he would have married and nothing would have happened. We could have forged a domestic affection amongst ourselves typically found in weekend TV shows, and our home would have felt a little more like home. I would have laughed at the unfounded, ridiculous premonition of my childhood as I looked back.

With each passing year, Grandma dropped by with three or four files and, oddly enough, they did not incite any impulse or weird feelings in me, so I left the decision entirely to Father. He continued to meet the women in the photographs, but none led to anything. Heavy workload and stress filled the empty space in his life, which resulted in many negative side effects, including his poorly directed primal needs. Grandma said that her son had to grow old a widower and end up in the hole because the dead bitch cursed him, and glowered at me.

Father brought that curse on his own head, and I have no regrets.

The shuttle bus arrived across the street just in time. People at the bus stop inched forward as they waited for the bus to make a U-turn and pull up at the station.

The bus pulled away and I saw a bakery that was hidden behind the bus. A girl in a blue shirt and an apron who was sweeping the shopfront looked up. She smiled and waved.

Who is she waving at?

I looked around, but no one was waving back at her. Everyone was craning their neck waiting for the bus to get here.

When I looked across the street again, the girl was leaning against her broom and smiling at me. No doubt we were looking at each other. But did I know her? Have I ever bought something from that bakery? No way. I hate bread. I'd rather have ramen. Even if

I did for some strange reason buy bread once or twice at that bakery, I wasn't a regular she would recognise and wave at.

I looked around me again. She was probably waving at someone passing by.

The bus turned around and pulled up at the station, blocking the view of the bakery again. I got on the bus, tapped my bus pass on the device, glued myself to the window and looked out, drawn by that inexplicable feeling I had that one other time. The feeling was a little different from the negative inkling I had when I glanced at the picture Father showed me. Back then, it was an intensely repulsive force that made me want to get as far away as possible, like two magnets of the same charge, but this was a strong pull, sort of like yearning.

Outside the bakery, the girl was still standing there. I opened the window and stuck my head out. The girl slowly turned around towards the shop, traces of her smile still lingering on her face. *Who are you? Why did you smile at me?*

'You there! Keep your head inside the window! It's dangerous!' yelled the bus driver.

The bus started with a loud rattle. I pulled my head back in, but my eyes were still on the shop. The door closed behind her as she went inside. I couldn't see beyond the display window. A college girl sitting by the window slammed it shut, annoyed by the wind messing up her hair.

Just then, an involuntary tear fell down my face. What was the meaning of this tear? Perhaps my life is missing something that used to be by my side long ago. What did I forget or lose? Were the girl and I close in some parallel universe I did not choose? I thought about all the elements and people besides her that I may have not chosen or flat-out refused in life.

The bus lurched and tossed my tears up in the air.

If No

'Water at table eighteen, and take their order. Move it!'

'Right away.'

At the manager's command, I put three cups of water on a brown, circular plastic tray and grabbed the menus. The manager seized my arm as I was leaving the kitchen and said in a low voice, 'Try not to talk if you can help it.'

'Yep.'

'How am I supposed to take the order if I don't talk?' I grumbled to myself as I hurriedly walked towards the customers.

At my interview for this temp job, the manager tried asking me a few questions and then quickly gave up. Instead, he asked me to get up, sit down, go left, go right, greet. He then asked his second-in-command to send all the other applicants away.

'If the waiter is tall, he tends to have a large build that can intimidate the customers, and a pretty face is a good thing, but you don't want someone too flamboyant. The important thing is how well the waiter goes with the interior decoration of the restaurant as he comes and goes about the place. Is he too jarring? Does he look out of place? Does it interfere with the customers' dining experience? So it is necessary that the waiter have the best body possible that makes the most of its sparing movement. The only problem is your speech defect. We'll figure it out as we go. Anyway, I'll have you know that the reason I hired you is because of your fantastically proportional body.'

That all sounded like bullshit to me, but I was surprised to learn that my body was perfectly proportional. Given that I lived on bread for years during an especially voracious phase in my life, it was amazing that I was nourished enough to grow as tall as I did. Perhaps the Wizard's Bakery breads really did contain some of Baker's special, suspicious ingredients that reached all corners of my body without my noticing and made me grow.

The 'speech defect' as the manager put it, got better little by imperceptibly little over three years. Since that day.

That day, when Mrs Bae jumped on me, I dropped the thing that was supposed to take me back to God knows when. I tried to get her off me, heard the crunch of the meringue under her foot, somehow got hold of her wrist, and got her to drop the eyebrow knife. Mrs Bae collapsed in a heap on the floor, completely spent after her fit of rage, and bawled.

Everything that happened since flashed past me randomly like a badly edited film. The police station, the TV station, the newsstands, Father fired, Father sentenced to two years in prison and three years on probation, the back of Mrs Bae's head as she went out the door around the turn of the season with Muhee's arm in one hand and a Samsonite trunk in the other, and repo stickers on all of our household goods. Our apartment ended up repossessed and up for auction in the process of shelling out lawyer fees and the divorce settlement. We had to vacate the apartment, and found ourselves a room on the first floor of a duplex as far away from the gale of redevelopment as possible.

On the last day at the apartment, I opened the small box about the size of a notepad.

Inside was the wax paper and plastic wrapper that contained the meringue pieces that Mrs Bae stepped on. It was completely pulverised so I couldn't find the finer pieces and put them back together. The coffee-flavoured chocolate paper slip with the date and time blank came out of the crushed meringue. I was right. Baker had given me the choice, even though an accident prevented me from using it.

The edible paper did not melt unless it came in contact with saliva or any other kind of moisture, so I had carefully wrapped it and kept it in the box. I thought about just eating the meringue pieces since he went through the trouble of making it for me and all, but I couldn't bring myself to eat what Mrs Bae stepped on. So instead, I had gathered the pieces and kept them safe. To remember that he gave me the strongest, most difficult-to-control power he could manage.

But when I opened the box, the meringue had turned grotesque with the chocolate paper disfigured and fused onto the meringue pieces. The inside of the box was lined with wax paper and plastic wrapping before I placed the meringue pieces and then the chocolate paper on top. But the rainy season and humid days continued, turning the box soggy and transferring the moisture to the plastic wrapper.

It was time to let it go. I finally made up my mind to burn it with the other thing, the voodoo doll that had been sitting in the freezer until yesterday.

Mrs Bae's rage and despair settled, and every last drop of her mental faculties were directed towards her plan to put Father behind bars when I presented the paper bag to her without a word. She looked inside and returned it to me contemptuously as if to say she didn't need this crap any more. She was not interested in finding out why I brought this to her, or what connection I had to the Wizard's Bakery.

After the Bae mother and daughter departed, I couldn't just toss the voodoo doll that looked exactly like me in the trash; there was a creepy superstitious energy emanating from it. I didn't know what else to do with it, so I kept it in the freezer instead. Even though Mrs Bae bought the doll to use it as my voodoo, I would have crushed it with my feet without any qualms if it looked like a generic man. But the doll looked so much like me that it was practically a work of art.

Even so, I didn't want to drag the voodoo doll into the new house and was wondering what to do with it when I saw the destroyed meringue.

Looking at it now, it felt as though all the spells I was under or the magic surrounding me had completely disappeared, even though it was, in fact, when the Time Rewinder broke, that the magic disappeared.

Two days after the situation hit rock bottom, I returned to the Wizard's Bakery and thought, *That was quick*. The store was empty, the glass door was wide open, exposing the vacant interior, and the sign was taken down. There was a piece of paper stuck to the window that read, 'Under Renovation'. Two workers were going in and out of the shop tearing down walls and peeling off the flooring.

So in the end, all that remained were my memories with them and the two things they gave me – a meringue cookie stripped of its magical powers and a voodoo doll made in my image.

The voodoo doll was cracked all over from being frozen for a long time, and when we emptied the fridge and unplugged it for the move, the doll defrosted in a matter of hours and a gaping hole formed where the small slot for the victim's hair or fingernail used to be. There was something strange about it. I thought it was a little light for a voodoo doll with its insides filled. Driven by some impulse, I plunged a box cutter in the chest of my replica. With a crunch, the marzipan collapsed beyond repair.

I looked down at its insides, dumbstruck, my vision blurring.

I set fire to a wad of paper in the bathroom sink. I put the sticky meringue into the fire and dusted all of its crumbs on top of it and finally dropped the hollow voodoo doll into the flames. The voodoo doll never contained any jelly or chocolate or anything that symbolised any part of my body. It was just a shell.

None of the articles and stories concerning Father mentioned his workplace or family by name, but the entire school discovered that 'A's son, B' was me. Rumours were distorted, broken up and reassembled. Before long, I was the infamous accomplice B who conspired with A to molest M. My body became the vessel of so much scorn and insult, and the places where its seeds were planted soon scarred.

The school understood that the police investigation proved I was innocent, but there was nothing more troublesome for the school than to keep an eye on a 'difficult student', so they cautiously suggested I transfer. I had to vacate the place and move anyway, so I gladly took their advice, no questions asked.

After the transfer, I slowly began to speak as though I was gradually being released from a spell I was under all these years. The progress was so slow one barely noticed, but vowels became words which became phrases as the years went on.

And three years passed.

The past, like a tangled ball of yarn, eventually straightened itself out.

I'd been strong so far, and I would continue to be. I knew that the accident that made the Time Rewinder unusable made me who I was today. My life may be like a piece of gum someone chewed and spat out, but I would endure it and extract every last molecule of sweetness from it.

When I brought out the pasta they ordered, one of the three women gave me her business card. The other two were sniggering and exchanging glances. I stood looking at them, trying to figure out what was going on.

'Come on. Take it,' the woman said with feigned irritation.

'Um, what . . . is this?'

'It's a business card.'

'But why . . . are you giving me this?'

'Are you in college?' The woman suddenly started

to speak informally to me. It didn't surprise me much
because customers complained about the bill or the
seasoning in their orders all the time.

'No.'

'Oh, you're still at school?'

'I . . . left school.'

'So it's not a felony, right?' she said as she looked at
her friends. 'Can I have your number? It could be fun,
yeah?'

I still had no idea what was going on.

'My number? What . . . why?'

'Not the sharpest tool, huh? I'm giving you my
business card to show you that I'm not some snake in
the grass trying to seduce you. I have a respectable job
at this company.'

I'd heard of married women in their thirties with
younger toy boys on the side, but I never thought I'd
actually see one in person. I gave her my business smile.

'I'm sorry. I cannot have personal relationships . . .
with customers . . . outside work.'

'Never mind. What a bore.'

The woman ripped her business card in two and
tossed it in the ashtray, too bruised by the rejection to
put it back in her card case. I put the ashtray on the
serving tray to empty it and bowed. 'Enjoy.'

I was returning to the counter when the woman
beckoned me again.

'Hey, you!'

'Yes?'

She tossed me something small in a plastic wrapper. Balancing the tray on one hand, I quickly grabbed the thing flying at me with the other hand.

'It's yours. For being pretty.'

'Oh. Thank you very much.'

I shoved it in my apron not knowing what it was. It was about an hour later that I went into the pantry and took a look at it. It was the end of the lunch-hour rush.

A mini castella? Why of all things . . . I hate bread.

The size and shape of it suggested that it was one of those samples they handed out at the subway station exits for promotions. I figured the women didn't want to eat it or throw it out, so decided to feed it to me for fun. *Please, no more assholes today*, I thought as I turned the mini castella over to look at the reverse side.

'Wizard's Bakery'.

Waves rose and fell like gills of a fish creating gentle ripples.

I tried to still my heart, telling myself that it could be a different bakery with the same name. I took a little piece of the castella and put it in my mouth. The taste confirmed I was wrong. At one point in my life, I ate their bread every single day, and no matter what it was, I would recognise his baking anywhere.

And what's more, the castella tasted of the Cheongn-yangni Station Peanut Cream Moon Bread I described to him just once through my impossible stutter. He'd recreated that uniquely personal taste I'd been seeking for years, the taste that brought me pain that felt so much like ecstasy.

If this isn't magic, what is?

Bolting out of the pantry, I rammed my thigh into the mini sink, knocked over a few bowls and the clothes stand, scattering staff clothes on the floor. Rubbing off the pain shooting up and down my leg, I came back out into the hall. I looked around for the people at table eighteen. They had just paid their bill at the counter and were on their way out.

'Wait!'

'Changed your mind?' The woman looked back at me.

'Ma'am, I'm sorry, but . . . where did you buy, the bread, you gave me?'

'Huh?'

I said 'buy' so as to not embarrass them, but that seemed to embarrass them even more.

'I'm sorry, but we didn't buy it. They were handing them out at the bakery that just opened up by the subway station.'

'Thank you so much. Have a great day!'

I gave them a ninety-degree bow. Their disappointed jeers floated above my bowed head. *What a weirdo. He's probably soft in the head.*

'What's going on?' The manager whacked me over

the head with a menu. 'Didn't I just remind you not to talk?'

'Um, sir, I apologise but . . .' I said as I took off my apron and put it over the back of the chair at the counter. 'Can I have, an early day? Just for today.'

'What? Hey! Are you sick?'

I had one foot out the door with my messenger bag hanging precariously on my shoulder.

'Hey!' the manager yelled. I looked back at him. He looked at me and the restaurant – he was probably thinking about my proportional body and its perfect match with the place's interior – and sighed.

'I don't know what this is about, but I'm giving you one hour. You don't come back in an hour, you're fired.'

'Okay!'

I rush down the stairs. I run. I run towards the subway station 600 metres ahead. I wonder what they will say when they see me now – they, who never grow old.

The voice of reason speaks in my head. Memories should be stuffed and preserved in a box. The box will gather dust and mould and moisture and be thrown out without a second glance someday. Fantasy is valuable only when it remains fantastical to the end. Returning to the place that once healed your wounds is not a way to move forward. You can't become an adult while holding on to the magic of your childhood.

But I ignore the voice and run even faster. Memories? Fantasy? All of those things had always been reality for me. Magic was never a detour that lifted me out of reality and into a land of dreams, but a matter of decisions.

I could see the Wizard's Bakery sign in the distance. Running like this, I am reminded of that day. I laugh. All those years ago, I reached their shop while desperately running from the reality crashing down on me.

But now, I run towards my past, my present, and the possibility of a future.

Author's Note

Requests? I'm not very picky. I don't even like sweets, and I unfortunately don't have a sophisticated palate to begin with. Just don't make it too sweet or heavy. No raisins or dried fruit of any kind. No red bean fillings if you can help it. I don't even like red bean bingsu in the summer. Chocolate's fine. Not milk chocolate, though. 56% cacao would be best. No peanuts or almonds for me, either. Nuts, I think, are fattening for the soul.

How about this: could you add something to erase the pain? Everything that I thought I'd gotten over and survived a long time ago that still seems to rear its head every now and then? And nothing that temporarily blocks the neural circuits. I want something that lasts. Permanent, if possible.

My pain is too abstract and subjective to treat? Well, that's too bad. I could give you an itemised list of things to erase, but that would keep us here all night.

How about this? I want something I can take tonight and wake up to a completely different reality. No?

How about little alterations in the sad circumstances of my life? If I'm being honest, what I want more than anything is brilliant sentences. If I can have that, almost anything else will be bearable. If I can have that, it'll be like a fresh coat of thick, cobalt blue paint on my weatherbeaten, discolored life. Could you add that spell to your confection? I could fill in the blank with so many things, but when it comes down to it, I want anything but what and where I am now.

He closed the recipe book where he was jotting down a list of ingredients, and set down his pen.

I'm afraid I can't help you, he said. I didn't ask why. I already knew the answer. Tell me, do you believe a small thing like this would change anything when you fundamentally cannot accept the present? Remember – there's only ever "now".

This is just a story about choices. Perhaps the odds are against us, perhaps life is nothing more than a baffling roll of the dice. Whichever the case, the consequences are ours alone to bear. I bet there are more people out there who have conceded to the flow of life, who merely suffer through it – more often than not living with baggage, without a home to return to, with bridges burned and never rebuilt. Because of that, I've unconsciously eschewed the narrative of homecoming and healing that lead to reconciliation and ends with visions for the future.

Without the support of the prize judges and editors, this novel would never have seen the light of day. To those who have tolerated me these long years and will continue to do so, I'm relieved their efforts have not been completely in vain.

Read on for an excerpt from Gu's brilliantly incisive
novel, YOUR NEIGHBOUR'S TABLE

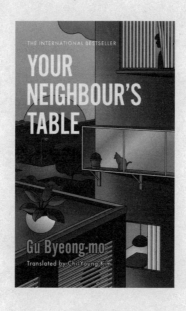

The backyard table was big enough to seat approximately sixteen adults, assuming you didn't mind brushing elbows with your neighbours each time you reached over to grab a napkin or a cup, big enough to squeeze in an additional half dozen kids if you packed in tight and didn't mind someone else breathing on you. This handcrafted table was too heavy even for four or five brawny men to pick up and move – its smooth tabletop was coated in varnish so glossy that you could almost see your face in it, its hefty corners were roughly hewn, and its legs, five thick pillars practically drilled into the ground, showed off the bumpy musculature of the wood used to make them. It was unknown who among the architects of this small apartment building had thought to install something like this in the backyard. But the table obviously wasn't an afterthought; a regular person with an ordinary job would never be able to afford such an extravagant custom piece.

With only seven adults and six kids, three of whom

were on their dads' laps, there was plenty of room around the table right now. It would become more challenging to accommodate everyone once all twelve units were fully occupied, but Yojin figured the families would rarely gather to eat as a group.

'All right, has everyone poured themselves a glass of wine?' Sin Jaegang, who had dashed out to greet Yojin's family the moment their moving truck extended its ladder to reach their windowsill, stood up. 'Welcome, Mr Jeon Euno, Ms Seo Yojin, and six-year-old Miss Jeon Siyul!'

'Welcome!'

'Nice to meet you!'

All the adults got up and raised their glasses, bowing in greeting, except for the dads with kids on their laps, who managed only to lift their arms. They clinked glasses and nodded at their neighbours across the table, and the kids imitated them, holding up their biodegradable plastic cups of tangerine juice before taking a gulp. Earlier, Jaegang had introduced Yojin and Euno to the other residents: 'Calling someone So-and-so's mom or So-and-so's dad is no fun at all, don't you think? Here we prefer to be called by our given names.' Now, reeling from the strangeness of hearing someone uttering her name outside of the doctor's or a government office, Yojin murmured her own name like an immigrant savouring the rarely used pronunciation of her native language, then ran her tongue across her gums.

Still holding his sleeping child awkwardly, Go Yeosan turned toward Euno. 'We thought you'd be tired after moving in, so we figured we'd just do some snacks and refreshments. I'm afraid it's not the most enthusiastic welcome.'

Euno's expression was grateful as he batted Yeosan's words away. 'Not at all. It's best to keep things simple. We aren't short-term guests or people who need to be wined and dined. We're just . . .' Here, he clinked his glass with Yeosan's without finishing his sentence; he figured he would come across as bristly, even if his tone were pleasant, if he said, *We're just the three newest residents joining this communal housing pilot program.*

The clinking of dishware, the murmur of conversation, and the whining of children hung in the early evening air. Gang Gyowon, Yeosan's wife, had pushed her glass away and was trying to feed their four-year-old son a late lunch. Even her flashes of irritation seemed to embody the pleasure of an affection-filled afternoon. Nobody coming across this scene would want to ruin this picture, this wholesome moment between mother and son. Living communally meant recasting noise as background music and messy scenes as frameworthy.

'Yojin-ssi, did you put the sheet of paper I gave you somewhere safe?' asked Hong Danhui, Jaegang's wife.

Yojin had only a faint recollection of accepting something from Danhui during the chaos of the move, but didn't let on that she was flustered.

'It's nothing too important, just some house rules,' Danhui explained. 'I wrote down the recycling days and things like that, so all you have to do is follow the schedule.'

Realising what Danhui was talking about, Yojin let out a sigh of relief like a bride who'd finished bowing to her new in-laws during the pyebaek ceremony. 'Oh, that's right. We're not fully unpacked yet, so I just stuck it on the fridge. I'll give it a read as soon as I get home.'

'Tomorrow's Sunday, so you have plenty of time. Anyway, Sangnak-ssi, is Hyonae-ssi super busy these days?'

Son Sangnak gave a brief nod and, preoccupied with giving his drowsy baby a bottle, muttered, 'Oh, she's always busy.'

Eight adults should have been present to account for every couple, but Yojin realised that Sangnak's wife wasn't there. *Oh, she's always busy.* It was an honest if terse response, possibly even insincere depending on how you looked at it. Maybe his answer was an effort to curtail the line of questioning, but Danhui added another weighted question.

'Even if she's on deadline, how hard is it to come out for a quick hello? We have a new family moving in. And you had to bring Darim out on your own.'

'It's just that she barely managed to meet her dead-line. She passed out right after. She didn't sleep at all the last three nights, so she won't wake up even if someone tried to haul her away right now.'

'Well. I guess there's nothing we can do if she's sleeping. Yojin-ssi, you're not upset, are you?'

'Of course not!' Yojin waved away the suggestion. 'Everyone has stuff going on, and we're no VIPs.'

As Euno had said earlier, they weren't guests and there was no need for formalities. Their relationship with their neighbours would be casual. In any other apartment building, they'd share a passing smile at most, and even now, having become a defined group of sorts due to the circumstances of their housing situation, knowing one another's names was more than enough. But the way Danhui kept needling Sangnak felt loaded; Yojin wasn't unaware of how the demand of 'a quick hello,' such small, seemingly trivial moments, could pile up and harden, encroaching on one's life. There were plenty of people who found it impossible to stand up for a quick greeting and plenty of situations in which doing the simplest thing for someone else was impractical.

On closer examination, Danhui, who appeared to be a few years older than Yojin, seemed like the type of person who would lead a women's association, driven by a preternaturally outgoing personality and love for appraising and organising various matters.

Yojin found it curious that someone like her had decided to live in such a remote village. This was the kind of place you'd move to in order to cut social ties, the kind of place where you measured quality of life by clean air and clean water.

'Now that your family has moved in, it finally feels like a community,' Danhui said, her tone friendly. 'I mean, it wasn't like we were lonely by ourselves or anything. But since Hyonae-ssi is some kind of free-lancer and works at night and sleeps during the day, it felt like there were just two of us women. It's great that we now have another! Let's have tea after we send our husbands to work and get to know each other.'

Yojin merely smiled, figuring she didn't need to correct Danhui right this second, but Euno spoke up. 'Actually, she's the one who goes to work while I stay home with Siyul.'

'Oh?'

Euno chuckled. 'I'm pretty unimpressive, so she's the one who works outside the home.'

Euno enjoyed using self-deprecation as a way to praise Yojin, but this habit of his sometimes made her feel awful, even though she knew he was trying to be nice. She didn't want him to cut himself down to boost her up – nothing sparkled in the light of comparative put-downs, and, more importantly, none of it ever sounded like a compliment to her.

'Oh . . . I see. So Yojin-ssi was making more, and that's why Euno-ssi decided to stay home.'

'Well, not exactly,' Yojin said vaguely, not wanting to get into how her husband was moping around like a bum after several of his films had fallen through, at least not during their first encounter with the neighbours. But she found herself worrying that Danhui might keep asking questions the way she had with Sangnak earlier, unable – or refusing – to read between the lines.

'Then Yojin-ssi – well, I'm not sure if I should ask you this when the unemployment rate is so high and it's so hard to get a permanent position, I mean, it's really hard for everyone right now – where do you work?'

Thankfully, the interrogation at least moved toward Yojin instead of staying on Euno. Though she didn't know why someone would say she wasn't sure if she should ask a question and then go ahead and ask it anyway, Yojin had at least expected this one, a question always added on like a surcharge whenever people learned that her husband stayed home and she went to work.

Euno beat her to it once again. 'She works at a pharmacy. It's right next to a neighbourhood pediatrician's office.'

'Euno-ssi, you're quite the spokesperson! You're not

letting your wife speak. So, a pharmacist! How impressive.'

Jaegang jumped in. 'Euno-ssi, you must be one of those lucky fellows we've heard tell of! A man whose wife provides for him!'

Yojin swallowed a mouthful of bitter, tart wine. 'No, I . . .' Yojin was reluctant to divulge too much about her personal life, but she was a firm believer in the power of clarity. It helped quash potential misunderstandings. 'I'm just the cashier.'

Yojin was an assistant to her pharmacist cousin, who had opened her own pharmacy. Her main duties were filling the prescriptions patients brought from the medical building next door, handing over herbal teas and nutritional tonics customers sought, and ringing up organic grain snacks and kids' vitamin drinks as well as bandages, masks, and other personal hygiene products at the counter. She also swept and mopped inside and out, cleaned the medicine cabinets and the shelves, sorted the trash, kept up with the inventory, checked manufacture dates, removed expired medications and reorganised them.

She wasn't a pharmacist or a specialist in medicine and didn't have a wealth of pharmaceutical knowledge, but she'd still memorised the active ingredients of commonly requested medications just in case, and, as a mother, learned the differences and the alternating dosages of Tylenol and ibuprofen; some of the tasks she handled technically violated the Pharmaceutical Affairs Act, but patients and guardians rarely took issue with her involvement, especially when there were hundreds of prescriptions to be filled in a day. Most importantly, she was efficient with the computer, and though it made her blood run cold to imagine misreading the name of a medication she gave a patient, she'd never made a grave mistake like that; she didn't even need to type in the correct spelling or chemical formula of a medication since she used a pharmacy-exclusive system that handled most of the process with a beep of the POS terminal.

If she were to amend any part of what Euno said, it would be the leisurely descriptor of 'a neighbourhood pediatrician's office.' As the pharmacy was in a bustling neighbourhood next to a medical building filled with all kinds of practices, Yojin didn't even have time for a lunch break on Mondays or on a day after a holiday. Still, they had it better than the pharmacy housed inside the medical building, which was busy enough to employ three pharmacists; she and her cousin could at least take breaks from time to time.

'Oh . . . I see.' Danhui was now embarrassed, and as she trailed off, Gyowon jumped in.

'What's wrong with working as a cashier? All that matters is working hard and making an honest living.'

'Of course not, there's nothing wrong with it!' Danhui recovered. 'I mean, I had a part-time job at the front desk of an English hagwon when I was a student.'

'That's just a part-time gig, so it's not the same as a real job,' Gyowon countered. 'A long time ago, when my mom told people she worked at K Apparel, people thought she was a designer and were impressed. She couldn't bring herself to tell them that she was a sales-clerk. Growing up, I always thought, what's wrong with retail? What's wrong with having only a high school degree?'

'Nowadays things are so different. You can get clothes at chain or discount stores if they're not designer,' Danhui said. 'It would be more like this – a friend told me that her daughter's classmate was brag-ging about how her dad worked at S Group. Turned out he was an AC technician for the subcontractor's subcontractor, going all the way down like a Russian nesting doll. Anyway, the point is, there's nothing wrong with being an AC technician. His business card has the same S Group logo on it, right? I told my friend it's basically the same thing.'

Yojin had only shared a few dry facts about her life, but her new neighbours were now going back and forth, assuming she was insecure about her job, taking turns digging up examples that were neither consola-tion nor encouragement. Yojin gave a curt nod and a wry smile. Her neighbours weren't the first to be sur-prised by the uncommon but increasingly less rare situation of a man staying home and his wife going to work. This had caused her to build up an inferiority complex, layer by layer, over the four years she'd been working for her cousin, a cousin she used to only see at weddings and funerals. She hadn't imagined that, even here, this would be the first question she would have to field; then again, it would be the same wherever she went. The only difference was the degree of people's nosiness.

'Take some time to really think about it first. Once you leave the city, it's going to be hard to make it back. Look what happened to me. The building boom in my planned city is over and things are getting bad. The prices in Seoul are so high that it's impossible for me to go back, but if I could . . . Still, I can at least get to Seoul by subway even if I have to make a transfer or two. What are you going to do out there in the middle of nowhere?'

This had been her friend's first reaction when she heard that Yojin and her family would be moving into the Dream Future Pilot Communal Apartments.

The Dream Future Pilot Communal Apartments was a small, twelve-unit building way out in the tranquil mountains without any urban amenities, a good distance from the homes that had been halfway developed about a decade ago during a modest building boom. At first glance, it appeared to be a random inn built on a vacant lot, without even a creek nearby. Still, it was brand-new and had been built with care by the government; it was clean and the decently sized units had a good floor plan, and, most crucially, it was public rental housing. But the conditions of residency were strict and you had to handwrite a pledge as part of the twenty-odd documents required for your application.

The ad seeking potential residents had claimed the building was 'just twenty minutes to city center,' but that turned out to be the same fiction as listings touting an 'incredibly transit-friendly area, three minutes to the subway,' which described every apartment Yojin and Euno had encountered since they got married. In reality, they would have to drive at least thirty-five minutes to even get close to Gangnam and Songpa, and there were no public transit options. Beyond the remote location and lack of infrastructure, the handwritten pledge was the most stringent requirement, and depending on your values, one of the prompts could be considered insulting. The pledge itself had fanned social media discourse; in the end, two hundred and forty couples applied for the twelve open spots. Those who made it through the review and interview stages were entered into a lottery, which didn't give preference to low-income families, but rather took into account current residential status and family situation and employment.

At least one adult in the family would have an impressive job, even if they worked on contract, and both adults probably held higher degrees than the average person. It wouldn't be at all unusual for at least several of them to be open-minded and progressive on various social issues while still susceptible to looking down on a cashier. Even so, the neighbours' words rattled in Yojin's ears and crushed her chest, and that sensation morphed into the conviction that she might not quite fit in here. She felt like a transfer student joining a classroom after the friend groups had already formed.

Yojin glanced at Siyul, wondering if her daughter was also feeling that way. Siyul was the oldest child here, and she was silently drinking her juice as she studied the other kids. Yeosan and Gyowon's son, Ubin, was now sitting between five-year-old Jeongmok and three-year-old Jeonghyeop, Jaegang and Danhui's two sons, and they were crashing their wooden cars together.

'Ubin, I told you to finish eating before you play,' scolded Gyowon, her irritation rising, and Yeosan whispered that she might wake Seah. In his arms, Seah was frowning, smacking her lips as she slept.

RAISING READERS
Books Build Bright Futures

Dear Reader,

We'd love your attention for one more page to tell you about the crisis in children's reading, and what we can all do.

Studies have shown that reading for fun is the **single biggest predictor of a child's future success** – more than family circumstance, parents' educational background or income. It improves academic results, mental health, wealth, communication skills and ambition.

The number of children reading for fun is in rapid decline. Young people have a lot of competition for their time, and a worryingly high number do not have a single book at home.

Our business works extensively with schools, libraries and literacy charities, but here are some ways we can all raise more readers:

- Reading to children for just 10 minutes a day makes a difference
- Don't give up if your children aren't regular readers – there will be books for them!
- Visit bookshops and libraries to get recommendations
- Encourage them to listen to audiobooks
- Support school libraries
- Give books as gifts

Thank you for reading.
www.JoinRaisingReaders.com